'The humour is ~~~~ously funny,
and more importantly relevant . . . like reading a
child's version of *Hitchhiker's Guide to the Galaxy*.'
Just Imagine

'Out of this world. Endlessly inventive . . .
will tickle and touch children's imaginations.'
Ian Whybrow,
author of *Harry and the Bucketful of Dinosaurs*

'Very different. Very funny.'
Jeremy Strong

'Very funny. Very good fun to read.'
Julia Eccleshare, *The Guardian*

'It is a hillarious book and I bet my family would
wet theirself if they read it. Well done!'
Charlotte (Year 6) Doncaster Book Awards

'Something funny and clever on every page . . .
astute observations on human life in all its
irrationality . . . Asquith's invention never flags.'
Books for Keeps

Ros Asquith started out as a photographer, became a theatre critic for *Time Out*, *City Limits*, and *The Observer* before emerging as a cartoonist. She draws regularly for *The Guardian* and has written and illustrated many books.

Ros lives in London with her jazz critic husband and two sons. She has stroked a tiger, cuddled a wolf, caught an escaped tarantula and juggled in a circus, but mostly prefers reading and eating fudge.

Find out more about Ros at www.rosasquith.co.uk

LETTERS from an ALIEN SCHOOLBOY

Galactic Poodle

Written and
illustrated
by Ros Asquith

Piccadilly Press • London

> Northamptonshire
> LRE
>
> | Askews & Holts | |
> | --- | --- |
> | | |

FOR

LOLA AND LENNY BRUCE

(and thanks to all at Piccadilly Press who,
despite being bumbling, mumbling, fumbling Earthlings,
have managed to make a silk book out of a pig's shorts)

First published in Great Britain in 2012 by
Piccadilly Press Ltd, 5 Castle Road, London NW1 8PR
www.piccadillypress.co.uk

Text and illustration copyright © Ros Asquith, 2012

Cover design by Simon Davis

ISBN: 978 1 84812 246 8
1 3 5 7 9 10 8 6 4 2

Printed in the UK by
CPI Group (UK) Ltd, Croydon, CR0 4YY

Galactic Poodle

EARTHLINGS, LISTEN UP!
You helped us vanquish our enemies the Threggs
with your amazing music.
You helped us destroy the Wiffly Biffly
with your amazing jokes.
But NOW another deadly threat approaches.
Do you have a third super power
with which to defeat them?
Shiver in your Earthling shoes and read on.

MISSION EARTH THREE: DAY ONE – SUNDAY

Measly Earth Dwelling Again
Row of Identical Dwellings
Titchy 'Country' Called England
Insignificant Blob Called Earth
Small, Dim Solar System
Forty-third Galaxy from the Right
Virgo Supercluster
Still at the Wrong End of the Universe

OK, Rok,

Here's the good news: as you can see we're alive.

The bad news is that instead of coming home to our lovely planet Faa, we're back on this foolish spaceblob, Earth.

You remember we were bringing Earth creatures back to Faa for the Emperor? They were all tiny because we had shrunk them with the amazing

Shrinker that my little sister Farteeta had built, so we could fit them into the spaceship.

But ten space tunnels were closed for repairs, so a journey that should have taken 45 Earth minutes took two Earth days.

Sharing a spaceship with grumpy gorillas, crazy cows and snapping crocodiles – even very small ones – is enough to drive you *bootglarked*, and the rats all got travel sick.

The KING of the JUNGLE Drowned in the VOMIT of a RODENT

Animals are such *snortblurking* liars and cheats!
The fox kept on begging us to let him share with
the chickens and rabbits.

'No! No! NO!' they shouted.

'Boo hoo, they are my BESTEST friends,' moaned
Foxy.

'Don't be mean – he wants to be with you,'
Farteeta said to the chickens and rabbits as she
opened the door to their cage. 'Be nice to him.'

'**NO!** You mustn't **BULLY** the poor little **FOX** Look how "**SAD**" and **LONELY** he is!'

But GULP, gnash, crunch, the fox scoffed two fluffy chicks and a baby rabbit before we could yank him out. He tried biting my left lower gripper, but I extended its protective shield just in time. His teeth went *kraaang* and he let out a furious growl.

Foxy is eating a hen! (But turn it upside down and then the hen is eating foxy.)

'*Splavoons,*' Farteeta said. 'He's growing back to his normal size – and so is Darren!'

Darren the lion, who had been the size of an Earth kitten when we shrank him, was already the size of a large Earth cat. Nellie the elephant's long curly beak was snaking into the cockpit round our dozy pilot Flyzoop's necks.

It was total chaos.

Bert, our robot, flashed and bleeped. 'ANIMAL EXPANSION ALERT! ACTIVATE SHRINKER!'

But, oh no! I had left the Shrinker behind with my Earthling friend Susan so she could keep a tiny horse as her pet.

'How did this happen?' squealed Mama as the biting, scratching, snarling creatures continued to expand, splintering their tiny cages and exploding into the spaceship. 'You said the animals would stay small for three days!'

'Space time continuum,' replied Bert, as if he

knew what he was talking about. 'Neglecting to pack Shrinker was a big boo-boo. Reverse to Earth.'

'Will reversing shrink the animals again?' I asked Bert, but he was too busy pushing Flyzoop out of the pilot's seat. Flyzoop was being useless and panicky as usual. Bert shot out a lower extender and kicked him in the sitting region.

'Owww!' wailed Flyzoop. 'Not FAIR!'

'Mission termination in four minutes, thirty seconds,' Bert droned. 'Prepare for evacuation of spaceship.'

'We can't survive without our spacesuits, Bert,' Farteeta squealed, 'and they're back there – past all those . . . those . . . things.' She pointed in horror at the ever-growing mountain of fur and legs and claws and teeth, growling and thrashing around in the main section of the spaceship.

'Bert can survive,' said Bert, glowing

brightly. 'I have plan to contact Earthling and retrieve Shrinker. If this does not work, will send message home saying no worries, all dead, sorry.'

'Thanks a lot, Bert,' we said, but he was busy operating a search on the communications database.

Earthling, Susan, female, friend

appeared on the screens next to a picture of Susan's unusually nice Earthling face.

I could hear an Earth phone ringing, and then a familiar voice coming over the speakers.

'Hello? Who's that? Hello?'

IT WAS SUSAN! Could she save us?

Bert started droning, `Earthling Susan, do not be alarmed. Please locate cell-growth inverter and proceed to latitude 51 degrees and —'

'Susan!' I shouted, grabbing the intercom. 'It's me, Flowk! The animals are expanding and we have to leave the spaceship. We're returning to Earth and will land in about three and a half minutes! Can you get the Shrinker and bring it to our house in that time? Otherwise we'll be eaten and a whole zoo will be rampaging round town.'

'What do you mean?' Susan squealed. 'I thought you'd gone home to another galaxy.'

'No time to explain! Can you do it?'

'I'll . . . I'll try . . .' Susan said.

`Entering Earth's atmosphere,' Bert burbled.

ABAAAAAAAndon spaceship. BAAAAck to Earth!

The ship was getting hotter, which made the expanding animals crosser still. A gorilla sprayed the fire extinguisher over Darren and an aardvark seemed about to bite its way into the cockpit.

Susan was still on her phone. We could hear her panting as she ran down the stairs in her house. We heard the front door slam. Would she make it?

'I can see you, I can see you!' Susan squealed down the phone. 'Ohmigoodness, you're on fire!'

RUMBLE

Oof. My stomachs are KILLING me.

RUMBLE

Moments later, we crash-landed in our garden,

The Shrinker

narrowly missing Papa's shed. The spaceship's door shattered and we all fell out, the animals on top of us. Farteeta screamed from underneath a hairy yak, Papa tugged a boa constrictor off his lower left gripper and Mama swatted a cloud of bats off her fourth head.

But hooray – brave Susan arrived just in time to save us, firing the Shrinker at the pile of arms and legs and heads and teeth. The Shrinker doesn't work on humans, so only the animals shrank. First their heads were reduced, then their bodies, legs, tails, wings and horns retracted until they were tiny again.

We all cheered. But instead of looking pleased, Susan looked up and screamed her one head off.

TERRIBLE Scream
ARRRGH

This is what she saw.

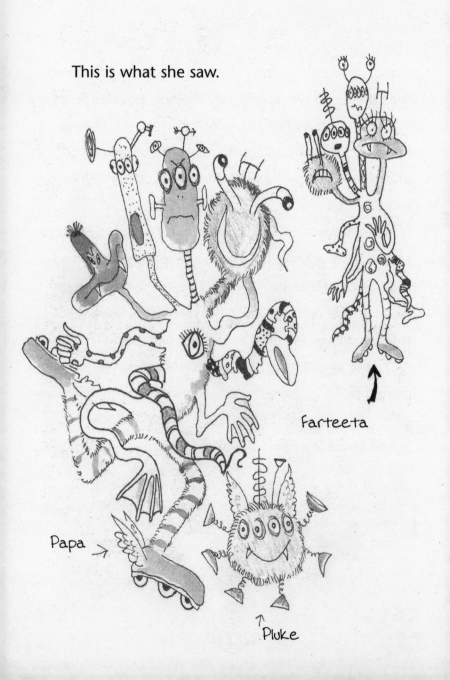

Farteeta

Papa

Pluke

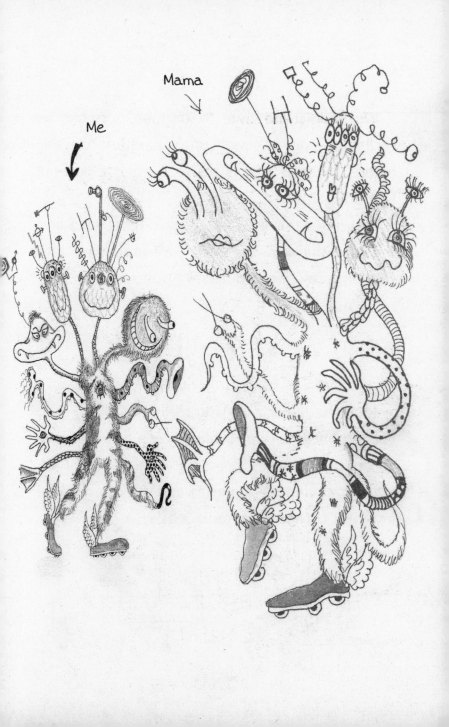

We hadn't had time to disguise ourselves as Earthlings and although she's seen us like this before, Susan is always scared by our handsome Faathing forms.

Bert raised the anti-matter shield to make us and the spaceship invisible while we transformed into Earthlings, by drinking massive doses of

I felt the familiar, sinking feeling of all my four beautiful heads – violet, blue, green and orange – collapsing into a single miserable, grey Earth face, while my whirlers, tentacles and suckers merged into near-useless 'arms' and 'legs'.

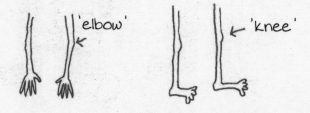

'elbow'

'knee'

I had forgotten, in just two days, how beastly it was. And I hate my Earth name: *Nigel.*

Mama flung us a pile of Earth clothes. Me and Farteeta were in a hurry and it's very difficult to get dressed in all these tubes and flaps. When we emerged from behind the anti-matter shield, what Susan saw was this:

Now she laughed. As you know, Rok, that's an Earthling sound like a hyperdrive engine trying to start with a dead *blooglewurg* squished in its converter. But it sounds nice when Susan does it.

I was so pleased she was happy that I looped over and hugged her. She screamed again. I'd forgotten to adjust the muscle sensors on my upper grippers and had crushed her a little. Susan is very good tempered however, which is another thing that makes her different from many Earthlings.

'It's good to have you back,' she said, smiling her nice smile at me. 'I've missed you.'

I liked that bit, Rok. More soon.

Yours devotedly,
Flowk

Dear Rok,

Capturing all the tiny
animals took ages.
The hens had shrunk
nearly as small as dear
little flies and one was

tragically stung by a bee. Meanwhile lions gobbled
lambs, a crocodile escaped into next-door's garden
and zoomed about in the pond eating the very

colourful fish that Colin Snell's dad is so proud of, and pigs danced in the compost heap. Oh dear.

Eventually Susan managed to pack them all in their cosy boxes, with plenty of food – apart from Henry the hippo who had become so friendly with a frog that she couldn't bear to pull them apart.

'Henry! Stop! Just think what odd younglings you'll have,' shouted Farteeta, to no avail. 'Perhaps that might be interesting, though.'

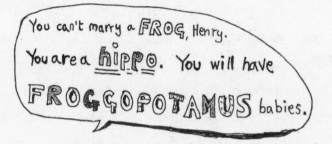

You can't marry a FROG, Henry. You are a hippo. You will have FROGGOPOTAMUS babies.

'Oh dear, I hope we haven't lost any animals,' said Susan. 'When the Shrinker wears off, they might eat someone.'

'Never mind,' said Papa. 'They'll stay small for a few days, which will give us time to fix the spaceship. Then we can get out of here for good and if some Earthlings get eaten no one will blame us.'

'You are so heartless,' said Susan.

'Completely incorrect,' Papa told her. 'We have four hearts to your one.'

Before Susan could reply, Bert squawked, `'Spaceship repair estimation false. Vehicle restoration time one Earth week minimum.'`

Flyzoop, who refuses to wear an Earth disguise, stayed in the cockpit snivelling. He looked like we felt. We were all sad that we'd be on this miserable, freezing planet for another week at least.

Just then, horrible Colin Snell's face appeared over the garden fence.

'Oh, hello, sonny!' shrieked Mama in her 'friendly' voice. 'Would you like to come over for a nice game of musical chairs? Or a jar of whisky?'

Colin snorted and disappeared. He will now tell everyone in my class at school that we are mad.

To make matters worse, Papa got this message from his boss at the Secretive Services:

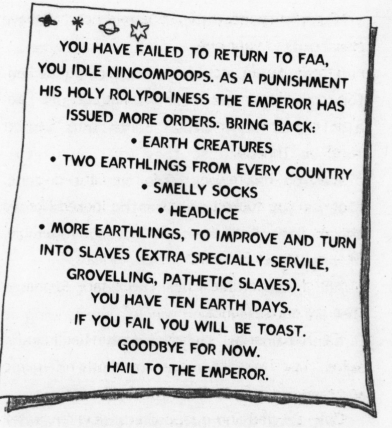

YOU HAVE FAILED TO RETURN TO FAA,
YOU IDLE NINCOMPOOPS. AS A PUNISHMENT
HIS HOLY ROLYPOLINESS THE EMPEROR HAS
ISSUED MORE ORDERS. BRING BACK:
- EARTH CREATURES
- TWO EARTHLINGS FROM EVERY COUNTRY
- SMELLY SOCKS
- HEADLICE
- MORE EARTHLINGS, TO IMPROVE AND TURN
INTO SLAVES (EXTRA SPECIALLY SERVILE,
GROVELLING, PATHETIC SLAVES).
YOU HAVE TEN EARTH DAYS.
IF YOU FAIL YOU WILL BE TOAST.
GOODBYE FOR NOW.
HAIL TO THE EMPEROR.

'The spaceship's wrecked, so there's a *sperkittelty* small chance of us getting home at all. And what *are* all these things?' Papa asked wildly.

Bert whirred his hyper messenger. 'Earth creatures already collected. Emperor requires two Earthlings from every tribe for language and research purposes. He also wants many other Earthlings which must be Improved so they will be useful slaves on Faa. Socks are the itchy foot clothes you have been wearing inside your shoes. Database does not reveal identity of headlice.'

'Ah,' I said, 'I recall learning about headlice. They are adorable-looking wingless insects living in Earthling hairstyles. They lay pretty white eggs called "nits" which incubate on Earthling heads and then hatch into more headlice.'

'Why would the Emperor want those? Or smelly socks?' asked Farteeta.

Bert fizzed, 'Never question His Holy Rolypoliness. Just obey.'

Papa had no idea what to do. Heads and tentacles zoomed out from his jacket.

Susan looked horrified.

'Don't worry,' I told her. 'He just needs to slurp *Vom* to stop his Earthling disguise slipping when he's stressed.'

Fi Fi –
next-door's poodle.

Mama put a gripper around Papa comfortingly, pouring a pot of *Vom* into one of his mouths. 'You must remember to take your hourly dose of *Vom*,' Mama warned him. 'We can't have your disguise slipping like that.'

'But how will we do everything in time to please the Emperor?' said Papa.

I hate it when Papa doesn't know what to do, Rok, and was trying to think of something brave and true when the doorbell rang. Colin Snell's dad marched in just as Papa's heads and tentacles had zoomed back out of sight.

'Where's Fi Fi?' he demanded. 'You've kidnapped her!'

He meant his pedigree poodle, who is the mother of my dear pet Pluke's puppies. Pluke adored Fi Fi just as she was, so of course we hadn't shrunk her.

Fi Fi squirmed under our sofa when she heard Mr Snell. He spotted her tail and yanked her out.

Pluke in his Earthling disguise as a dog.

'So sorry,' squealed Mama, 'but Fi Fi keeps coming round to our house. What can I do? Please join us for a kettle of gin and an onion or two.'

'You're barking,' said Mr Snell, holding on tightly to Fi Fi.

'Isn't barking what dogs do?' said Mama after he'd gone.

Pluke was inconsolable. He hates being disguised as a dog called Rhubarb, but he loves Fi Fi.

'You've still got your nice two-headed puppies,' I comforted him. 'They're safe upstairs.'

'But I don't have my fluffy poodly woodly Fi Fi,' whined Pluke.

To escape all this *flaarfing* and moaning, I walked Susan back to her house.

'Finding smelly socks and headlice will be easy,' she said, 'but how are you going to gather two people from every country? Have you any idea

how many countries there are?'

'You Earthlings are too dumb to know the answer,' I said. 'Some of you say 196, others say 205 – and oddly you have over 6,000 different languages . . .'

'How do you *know* all that?' said Susan, her eyeballs stretched wide.

'Faathings know almost everything,' I said. 'We have roughly 8,347 times more intelligence than you. But we don't know of other planets divided into different countries, which must be why the Emperor wants to find out more. I can easily fly round the world in a single night. Why don't you come with me?'

The thought of a world trip with Susan made my hearts expand, but she looked thoughtful.

'You mustn't take people unless they want to go with you, Nigel,' she said quietly. 'They're human beings, with their own lives and people they love.

It would be magic to fly with you, and see them all, but you can't steal them for your stupid Emperor to play with.'

'He's not stupid. He's a master of the Universe. And he'll vaporise us if we don't do what he says,' I replied.

'It's a horrid idea, Nigel,' Susan said firmly. 'You must promise me you won't do it. I won't ever be your friend again if you do.'

'But Faathings must obey their Emperor,' I said.

'Tough,' she said, tossing her hairstyle. 'Count me out.'

So I counted, though I'm not quite sure why. I had only got to ten million, which took me just two Earth seconds, when I realised she had gone.

It's now midnight. I was just drifting off to sleep while thinking of a plan to convince Susan to fly around the planet with me, when I heard Bert wailing.

'Where is Bertina now that I need her? Where oh where is my pudding, Bertina?'

I crept up to his study. He trundled back and forth, sending up showers of sparks.

'Bert,' I whispered. 'You're . . . surely not crying, are you?'

'Robots never cry. Only feeble Earthlings emit eyeball H_2O.'

But he continued to fizz and splutter till he was howling like an Earthling baby.

I ran to find toilet roll (that Earthlings use to wipe their poo poos). Repulsive, but I did what must be done.

'You must stop cry—, I mean noising, Bert. You'll short-circuit.'

I reached to pat his blue plastic skull. He sniffed (I'm not sure how, for he doesn't have a beak) and drank a whole kettle full of engine oil.

'We should never have programmed you to

have feelings, Bert,' I told him. 'But if you don't mind my asking, who is Bertina?'

Bert's skull glowed crimson. '**Skirt cleaner? Why would I be interested in skirt cleaner?**' he bleeped.

Perhaps I'd misheard him and he is homesick, just like me.

'Do you think we have a chance of getting back to Faa soon?' I asked him.

Usually Bert comforts me when I'm worried, but all he did was sigh.

So here I lie on my hard Earth bed, wondering how to make my best Earthling friend Susan take a wonderful flight with me. I'm sure there's a way.

Your friend in science,
Flowk

Rok,

Discovering Earthling music may have saved us from our enemies the Threggs, but when I hear Mama 'singing', I sometimes wonder if it was worth it.

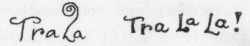

she goes, like a Wiffly Biffly just before it eats you. 'Spidoodle bardle bee, put the kettles on. Toodly scoot badaddly, let's pop some carrots in the hoover. Bongy boodle wackety poo, time to toast some CDs.'

This morning she was reading a 'magazine' about 'film stars', which are well-known Earthlings, not astral stars. She keeps telling us which film star has got married or bought a big new house. 'Film stars are the most clever and powerful female Earthlings,' she says. Papa is worried she is developing the very worst Earthling habits.

In between burbling about film stars, she was mixing washing powder and the Earth cow juice they call 'milk' to clean our portholes, despite Bert telling her to use H_2O.

'You do your job and I'll do mine, tiddly pom,' she told Bert, busily rubbing the frothy white stuff all over the glass. Then she started wiping them 'clean' with the bedclothes. (Did I mention that Earth beds wear clothes, just like humans?)

It is now very difficult to see out of the portholes, not that there was anything worth looking at in the first place.

Tiddly Pom! Tra La La!

This bed clothe is called a 'doovay'.

'Back to being an Earth housewife,' sang Mama. 'I'm beginning to enjoy it. Although if I were a film star I would have a servant to do it. Never mind, I'll put on my apricot and dust the garden.'

'It's not an apricot, it's an apron,' said Papa, 'and you could try dusting in here first.'

He gazed gloomily around our 'living room'. Everything on Earth is covered in a fine layer of  dust, Rok – which, I'm sorry to say, is made up mostly from human skin. They just leave it around wherever they go.

'Time for school,' said Mama. 'We must behave as much like a normal Earthling family as possible. I must admit I'd prefer to be in a nice film star's mansion, but never mind. Papa will sort everything out for the Emperor. Papa knows best.'

But I am beginning to realise he doesn't, Rok. Papa seems really confused and it is making me sadder than a *spongoon*.

It was still raining down little snowballs from a dark sky as I walked to school.

On my way I noticed an ancient Earthling tussling with a large green vegetable. I did not know vegetation on Earth fought back, but I whizzed to the rescue, pulling the spiky green thing off the old person and flinging it into  the path of a passing bus.

Instead of thanking me, the old Earthling used some very rude words and said I had destroyed her 'Christmas tree'.

I thought it was most ungrateful but couldn't stay to argue as I was by now late for school.

The first thing I did when I got there was memory-blast my friend, Roddy, so he forgot that I was an alien. Apart from Susan, he was the only Earthling who knew the truth. Other Earthlings seem to think Roddie's odd because he's always flapping his arms and making strange sounds. They don't seem to realise they're all just as odd as him. I know no one will believe him if he tells them I'm an alien, but they might think he's *bootglarked*, which they call 'mad', and put him in prison. Earthlings are not kind to people they think are mad.

'Now we have exciting rehearsals for a pantomime,' said our teacher Miss Barn in the first lesson. 'We were going to do *Cinderella*,' she continued, 'but unfortunately our papier mâché coach was recycled by the caretaker, so instead we will do *The Frog Prince*. Roddy has agreed to write some songs, haven't you, Roddy?'

Roddy appeared to be making a paper hat for

his pencil. He likes collecting things. Last week it was sweetie wrappers, this week it is pencils.

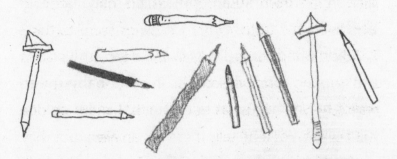

Some of Roddy's pencil collection.
So far, he has only made two paper hats.

'YES, Miss Barn,' he bellowed. (Like Mama, he can't control his volume.) 'Croaking songs for FROGGIES. And a pencil chorus. I will compose it in the key of B for the HBs. Then in F sharp.'

Miss Barn rolled her eyeballs and told us the history of *The Frog Prince.*

A baby queen wandered away from a 'castle' where she lived with the mummy queen and king.

All the king's horses and all the king's men looked for her, but she foolishly dropped her valuable golden football into a pond, which made her eye-balls water.

I didn't understand why she was sad, so I put up my gripper and said, 'But if she is a baby queen won't her mama be able to buy her more golden footballs?'

'Stop interrupting, Nigel. She is a princess and is saved by a frog, as you will see, if only you will sit still and listen.'

I knew a frog was a small, hopping, croaking Earth amphibian like the one our hippo wanted to marry, and was interested to see how such a small pet could save a princess, so I listened carefully.

The frog, it turned out, popped up from the pond carrying the football in its flippers. It must have been a very big frog, or a very small football. Anyway, the princess was so happy to see her

X

X   X

X   X   X   X   X

X   X

Oddly, Rok, this symbol means 'wrong' and also means 'kiss'.

football again that she 'kissed' the frog. Kissing is a disgusting-looking wet splattery thing that Earthlings do with their mouths to show they like each other.

I'm not sure how it worked, but when this princess kissed the frog, there was a big flash and behold! The frog turned into a baby king (or 'prince')! And they married and were very happy ever after.

I was amazed, Rok. I had no idea that Earth creatures could transform like that. I couldn't wait to get home to try it out on our frog. Also, something strange was happening to my hearts to hear that the baby king and queen were so happy. My Earthling eyeballs were watering too, so Susan offered me a bogey tissue to dry them. Naturally, I refused.

'A little bird flew into my eyeball, that's all,' I said.

'You mean an insect,' Susan said, wrinkling her beak rather sweetly. 'You are hopeless, crying at a *fairytale*,' she added.

Then Miss Barn made us read bits of *The Frog Prince* out loud, not in our own voices, but as if we really were the frog or the king. It's called a 'play', which means pretending to be somebody else. Colin Snell and Jatinder were the king and queen in the castle while the rest of us were soldiers marching about shouting:

'Oh dear we are in great distress,
where oh where is our little princess?'

Then we pretended to be the pond, lying on the floor wiggling, while Annie Spratt rolled about being the beautiful golden football. We were supposed to go 'SPLASH' when she rolled near us, but everybody was laughing too much to say it. Aaron Ratchett kicked Annie Spratt and shouted 'GOAL' instead. Aaron then pretended to be the frog and Susan was the princess. When she kissed him, everyone went 'YUK', but I felt cross, because Susan has never kissed me.

Aaron Ratchett does look
very like the croaking Earth
amphibian known as a 'frog'.

Despite that, it is fun doing plays, Rok. I will show you how when I get home to Faa.

Double science was next, and Miss Barn taught us the names of the planets in Earth's solar system. Her trick for this went, 'My Very Easy Method Just Speeds Up Naming Planets' – with each word sharing the same first letter as

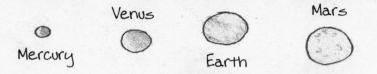

Venus

Mercury

Earth

Mars

Mercury, Venus, Earth, Mars, Jupiter, Saturn, Uranus, Neptune and Pluto. I put my gripper up to say it didn't work any more because Earthlings reclassified Pluto in 2006 as not a true planet but only a dwarf planet.

'Instead you could say My Vast Elephant's Mum Just Sells Underpants Now,' I added helpfully, although Miss Barn frowned when everyone giggled. I tried to cheer her up by telling her how to remember the names of the 96 nearest galaxies. I thought this would be fine, since even hopeless Earthling scientists have used infra red light to plot 50,000 galaxies in the nearby universe, but just as I was starting my explanation, Jatinder interrupted.

'Nigel's really odd. Do you think he's from another planet?' she asked.

'Don't be unkind, Jatinder,' said Miss Barn. 'Anyway, alien life might exist, but it's too far away to visit us.'

Jupiter

Saturn

Uranus

Neptune

'That's not true, Miss Barn,' I said, unable to stop myself even though Susan was giving me a warning look. 'Intelligent life exists in at least 200 galaxies, and there have already been many visits to Earth.'

'He's right, Miss,' Aaron Ratchett said. 'Haven't you watched *Doctor Who*?'

'You've both been reading too much science fiction,' said Miss Barn, looking at me with very narrow eyeballs.

'Serves you right, Big Head,' whispered horrible Colin Snell.

Big Head? I was suddenly worried that my Earthling disguise was slipping and my face was no longer the correct size. I asked if I could go to the boys' toilets. You may remember, these are the pieces of furniture Earthlings visit to do poo-poos and wee-wees because their bodies are so inefficient that they don't absorb all their food.

I checked my head size in the mirror. Relief – it

seemed to be OK. By great good fortune, there were a lot of shoes and socks piled up outside the toilets. I took the socks, which luckily were all very smelly, and put them in my schoolbag. Papa will be proud of me.

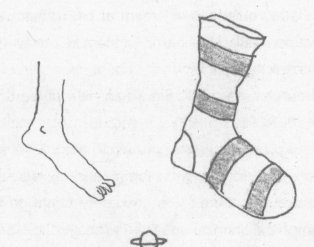

To see the Earth foot go into the smelly sock, move the page towards you until your beak touches the planet.

I came back to our dwelling to find Bert in a happier mood for some reason. He told me that someone was coming from Faa with spare parts for the spaceship. He had obviously been worried about not getting it repaired in time.

At least it is comforting hearing the tiny animals snuffling quietly in my room at night. Susan's little pet horse, Blackie, has joined them because we have to keep the Shrinker at our house now. I am pleased about that, too, as I think Susan will visit more often.

Poor Farty's been at playgroup where she has to be an Earthling three-year-old called Sultana. It's very hard for her to pretend to be as stupid and ignorant as them so she was very happy to try to adapt the Shrinker as soon as she got home. I told her I'd need it to work on humans as well as animals, so I can capture people from other countries.

'That's fine,' said Farty. 'Earthlings aren't superior beings like us so a few adjustments should do it.

I have several thousand pages of instructions.'

'OK, Farty,' I said, 'but before you take it, I'll just fire it at the animals. I'll do it every day, in case they start expanding again . . .'

'You're such a *faarfler*. If you shrink them too often they might disappear,' snorted Farty.

But I'd already pressed the trigger. Luckily, the animals just stayed the same small size. The hippos reminded me of my *fluit* collection back home.

Miss you a bit, Rok.

Flowk

Oh I miss my little juggling fluits. Please make sure they are kept at boiling temperature and have plenty of acid and mercury.

Dear Rok,

I was woken at midnight yet again by weird sounds from Bert. I sneaked into the corridor and there he was, his normally blue plastic skull bright pink, all his lights glowing, and his great metal arms clasped tight around – *splavloons!* – another robot!

'Bertina, my dumpling! My puddingy plumpling! My all, my basket of treats,' he was squeaking.

Bertina was quite something – twice the size of Bert, with four more arms and made up of many colours. I wish I was on Faa, where I could see all her colours properly. Earth light is very limiting and only reveals a fraction of the universal colour spectrum. Bertina sprang back from Bert, raising six of her arms and turning her central flashlight on me.

'Howdy doody kid, I am Bertinaweenacuppateenaevaseenasweetaqueenaoooooompus,' she said. 'I've dropped in from Faa with some neat stuff to fix up your spaceship.'

I gazed admiringly, and so did Bert, who had now gone a very deep pink from the top of his skull to his rollers. Soon Mama, Papa and Farty had all gathered to see what the commotion was about.

'Welcome to you, sir,' Papa said, and Farteeta rolled her eyeballs. Papa does tend to assume that anyone useful is male and this seems to annoy her. 'Good to see a 68th generation robot. Now we'll finally get some proper work done.'

akaime

Bert's lights dimmed and his extenders drooped forlornly.

'Well, hi,' said Bertina in a low voice that made me think of Earth honey and hot engine oil mixed together. Her lights grew brighter and she shook her multi-coloured plastic head from side to side, making a little tinkling sound. I realised the noise was coming from gold metal objects attached on each side.

'Earrings,' whispered Mama in wonder. 'I've seen them in Earthling magazines. They are worn by film stars. I've been longing to wear some.'

'You can borrow my spare pair, Big Mama,' Bertina purred, handing some to her. 'I reckoned if I was coming to Earth, I'd better blend in.'

It was amazing how Earthling-like she sounded – nothing like Bert. Her voice was a bit like Adam One's and he is from an Earth country called America. The robot programming must have advanced since Bert's time.

Mama and Farteeta clapped their hands. I don't know why – it's not as if Earthlings weren't going to notice Bertina was a robot just because she talks like that and wears earrings.

'I left my galaxy-cruiser in your front yard,' Bertina said. 'Hope that's cool.'

I was about to agree that it was indeed cool – in fact, very cold – outside, but Papa looked horrified and ran to the window.

'A Faathing galaxy-cruiser?' he muttered. 'How are we going to explain that?'

But it wasn't a Faathing galaxy-cruiser. It was a huge pink Earth car, but not like any I'd seen before, with long silver fins at the back. Bert's lights blinked as he whirred through his Earth databank.

'Cadillac Eldorado, 1953, manufactured Detroit, Michigan, USA,' he announced.

'Groovy disguise for the cruiser, ain't it, Daddy-O?' Bertina said, brightly.

![Papa says Bertina's Cadillac has too many aerials and will arouse suspicion.](illustration of a Cadillac with many aerials)

Papa says Bertina's Cadillac has too many
aerials and will arouse suspicion.

'This is London, England, in the twenty-first
century,' Papa said. 'It's about as conspicuous as
a non-disguised galaxy cruiser, especially in that
ridiculous colour.'

'Oh, don't be such a party pooper, Big Daddy,'
Bertina said, pushing Papa playfully with an extender
and sending him crashing into a cupboard. 'Oopsy.
Now, let's get with it. I bring spare parts for your

ship, Bad News and after that, Even Worse News.'

'Could you tell us the Even Worse News first?' Mama enquired. 'Then the Bad News won't seem so bad.'

'Sorry, babe,' Bertina crooned, 'not sure you guys are strong enough to hear it.'

'You boring robots,' said Papa, sounding really cross. 'We are Faathings of the True Breed, we don't have to listen to you.'

Bertina and Bert together set up such a bleating and bleeping and hooting and parping and bibbling and bobbling and swooshing and *finoodling* that we couldn't hear ourselves think.

'Shut up!' Papa yelled. Amazingly, they both did.

'OK, no need to flip your lid. Here's the Even Worse News,' Bertina finally said, with Bert comfortingly enfolding her left titanium investigative probe in his own. 'Something terrible is about to attack this dullsville old planet.'

The dreaded Threggs are returning.

'Noooooooooo!' we all wailed.

'As usual, those oddball Threggs have a tentacle in it,' Bertina said. 'We picked up a message from Keith, King of Threggs, after he'd found out you Faathings were back on Earth. You wanna hear it?'

Bertina's speaker-system blared. It was a horribly familiar voice:

HOO HAR.
VILE FAATHINGS HAVE RETURNED.
BUT WE WILL MINCEMEAT MAKE THEM.
ELIMINATED THEY WILL BE AND ALL
WHO DARE TO STICK TONGUES OUT
AND FACES MAKE AT THE
GLORIOUS ARMY OF THREGGS.
SUMPTUOUS SPINACH SHALL TRIUMPH.
WET ONES ARE
ON THE MOVE.
MANDY SHALL PREVAIL!'

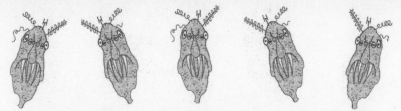

'CRAZY translation, we're still working on it, but you get the picture, dahlings,' said Bertina.

'I'm not scared of stupid old Keith,' Farty said. 'We've defeated him twice already. But who's Mandy?'

'There's a girl called Mandy in Year Six at my school,' I said. 'Is she a baddy in disguise?'

'Unlikely. Our translators think it might stand for . . .' Bertina paused. '. . . Mince, Annihilate, Nuke and Destroy Younglings.'

'Nooooooooooo!' we said again, shivering.

'These "wet ones" are so rare and so evil they're not even in the Encyclopedia of Predators,' Bertina continued, 'but we reckon they may be . . . BODY SNATCHERS!'

'Body Snatchers?' we all said.

'Yeah. We've found out that, like us, they can disguise themselves as Earthlings,' Bertina explained. 'But, unlike us, they have to copy an existing being. So you couldn't tell if, for instance, the Prime Minister was an Earthling or a Body Snatcher in disguise. Then, once they've disguised themselves and snooped around a bit pretending to be human, they phone home and their buddies arrive and flood the whole planet.'

'But why would they do that?' I said.

'We ain't sure yet, but we guess they like to be WET.'

'And you're sure they're coming here?' Papa asked.

'Yes indeedy, super speedy,' Bertina said, her warning lights flashing. 'So the Bad News is you all gotta get headlice, smelly socks, people from every country, and more Earthlings real fast. And then skidaddle. LOTS to do, Big Daddy,' she whirred. 'I've only got a two-seater, so we've also gotta repair your ship AND Improve the

Improver that you guys built last time you were here.'

'For what?' Papa asked.

'To Improve the Earthlings so they'll make good slaves on Faa, obviously,' Bertina said.

An idea came to me then. I thought Susan just might agree to fly round the world with me if I could persuade her it was in a good cause . . .

'Let's get moving, kiddos,' Bertina said. 'Flowkmazzabumius,' – it was strange to hear Papa being called his proper Faa name – 'the parts for your spaceship are in the boot of the Caddy, I mean, galaxy-cruiser. You and Bert are in charge of mending that.'

She turned to Mama. 'Bumeflowkmissus, you round up as many people as you can to come round when the Improver's been rebuilt. We need to make them a bit more intelligent, add a few heads and tentacles and erase their feelings. You gotta get with it and make friends.'

'What fun!' Mama said, glancing at her new earrings reflected in Bertina's chrome plated extender. 'I was really getting the hang of it before. It will be a doddle deedle, tra la la! I could ask all your friends' parents to tea,' she said to Farty.

Farty groaned and whispered to me, 'I know Mama tries hard to behave like a normal Earthling mother but she's SO embarrassing.'

'We'll just have to keep our eyeballs on her,' I whispered back.

Bertina was now talking about rebuilding the Improver and disguising it as an Earth bank.

'Earthlings WORSHIP money, so they'll be crazy for it,' Bertina explained.

'Earthling banks discredited since Earth year 2008,' Bert said. 'Suck up Earthlings' money, pour down drain.'

'Not this bank, dahling,' Bertina said, shaking her tinkling earrings. 'This one don't take, it gives. There ain't barely no money left on Earth, so it'll be groovy.'

'Easy peasy, tra la la lee,' screamed Mama. 'Bert's printer makes a million ten pound notes every minute, tra loo dollar diddle! So Earthlings who visit the Improver will be million airs, just like gorgeous, clever film stars.'

'Too right,' said Bertina. 'You sure are smarter than you look, Big Mama.'

Mama looked pleased, then cross, then pleased again.

Turn Mama's happy face upside down to see her sad face.

'Farteeta and Flowkwee, you guys gotta hunt for smelly socks, Earthlings from different countries and headlice,' Bertina continued. 'Sorry about that, kids.'

'I have 56 socks already,' I said, pulling the ones I'd found at school out of my bag.

Bertina extended a smell-sampler to scan them, and wobbled backwards on her rollers.

'Woweee-zowee, just like the perfume worn by the Emperor's favourite wife. I guess that's why he wants them,' Bertina said, withdrawing her smell-sampler hastily.

'The headlice, by the way, are gonna be her pets. I heard she eyeballed them on the

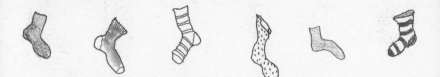

Interplanet and kicked up her tentacles squawking, "I want my incy wincy littly bittly nittly wittly LICE. And I want them NOW!"'

So that explains the socks and the headlice, Rok. I'm determined to persuade Susan to come round the world with me as soon as possible. Farty swears she's fixed the Shrinker now so it works on people too.

'Are you sure?' I asked her as we went back to bed.

'Well, it worked on Mr Snell,' she said. 'Look.'

She opened her gripper and there was Colin's dad, jumping up and down squeaking, 'Fire! Ambulance! Police! Giants!'

'He's quite sweet now, isn't he?' she said. 'Let's keep him that way.'

But I panicked. 'It'll take him three days to grow big again, and by then they'll have the police searching for him. They might come here and find the animals! You should have asked me before you used the Shrinker.'

'Oh, keep your stupid Shrinker if you're so clever,' said Farty. 'I thought you'd be pleased.'

'Sorry, Farty,' I said quickly. 'It's *very* clever of you to have adapted the Shrinker.'

'It's OK.' She smiled. 'There's always the reverse setting. Have you got the Memory Blaster ready?'

I nodded (much less effective with only one head) and she put the squeaking midget on the floor, pressed Reverse on the Shrinker and then fired it at him. Up burst a very cross Mr Snell.

I memory-blasted him and politely asked, 'What can I do for you, Mr Snell? Are you looking for Fi Fi again?' as I led him out of our dwelling and back to his own.

Anyway, I must go to sleep if I am to cope with school in the morning. I've fallen asleep there before because my brains were so bored. Luckily it was during geography so I was not the only one.

Great news! At school today I told Susan about the Body Snatchers. I let her get quite scared so I could put a comforting arm around her. 'But don't worry,' I said, 'that's why the Emperor wants us to capture two people from each country – so that we can persuade the whole world to agree on a plan to defeat the evil Body Snatchers. AND we'll make all the poorest people into million airs with a new bank we are building.'

'Really? Are you sure?' said Susan.

'Yes,' I told her. I know it wasn't quite true, Rok, but it seemed to be the only way to convince Susan to come with me.

There was a long silence in which all my hearts beat like a flock of *spogoons*.

Then Susan said, 'If we can get all the people of the world together – the ordinary people, not the leaders – then perhaps we can not only defeat the Body Snatchers, but have world peace too.'

'Yes, that's the general idea,' I said.

'Oh, please can I come?' Susan begged.

'OK, if you really want to,' I said, as if I didn't care. I've noticed that Earthlings often want to do something more if they think they might not be able to.

So, I've checked with Papa and we will go tomorrow night. Wish me luck.

Yours in hope, as ever,

Flowk

I am returning your mindscan of Pluke's friend Skab. I don't want to hurt her feelings, but Pluke's hearts beat only for Fi Fi now. Sorry.

MISSION EARTH THREE: DAY FOUR – WEDNESDAY

My dear friend Rok,

As soon as I got to school I told Susan we could go flying tonight. She was as excited as I was.

I didn't think I'd be able to concentrate on anything at school today, but I was wrong. We did something called 'rehearsing' for *The Frog Prince*. I almost gave my true identity away, I enjoyed it so much.

We started with an 'audition', which meant showing how well you can pretend to be the character, so you get chosen to play that person.

Susan had been picked to be the princess so I thought I'd try to be the frog.

'Yah!' shouted Colin Snell. 'Ugly and slimy, you'd be perfect!'

'You'd be better,' said Aaron Ratchett. 'Big holes in your nose. And poppy eyes.'

Colin Snell fell on Aaron Ratchett and they rolled around on the floor.

I said, in my frog voice.

Colin Snell and Aaron Ratchett stopped fighting, and Miss Barn stared at me.

'That was very good, Nigel,' she whispered. 'Do it again.'

I said deeply. An accurate frog voice is very easy with our eighteen vocal cords, Rok. I don't know what all the fuss was about. But, as usual, I got carried away. I was concentrating so hard on frogs that my lower rear whirlers shot out, bent, and sprang open so fast nobody saw *them*, but everybody saw *me* flying right over Miss Barn's head, narrowly missing the classroom ceiling, and landing on Orville Muffin's desk.

'Wow,' said Adam Two. 'Frog power.'

'Catch the fly, Froggie,' Jatinder yelled, grabbing Annie Spratt's lunchbox and spinning it towards me. Without thinking, I activated a hidden upper extender, fired it out of the top of my 'shirt' and caught the lunchbox when it had almost passed my head. I then twirled it back so it landed neatly inside Annie Spratt's schoolbag.

'Result,' said Aaron Ratchett. 'Frog one, fly nil.'

'He's an alien!' shouted Jatinder.

'No he's not,' said Susan. 'He's just very fit.'

I have heard Colin Snell say Susan was very fit too, so it was nice to be similar to her.

'Well, I don't know about you,' said Miss Barn brightly, 'but I think that makes Nigel the Frog Prince.'

'Nigel's a frog, Nigel's a frog!' everybody cheered.

'And now we need someone to be the prince,'

Miss Barn continued, 'after he is transformed.'

'Surely that will be me too, won't it?' I asked. 'It's still the same person inside.'

'No, we must have parts for everyone. You can't be both,' said Miss Barn.

Oh dear. I did want to be in the scene where he marries Susan. Instead, I contented myself with the thought that I'd have Susan to myself all evening.

Farty also had a good day at play-group. She had rubbed heads with all the younglings she could find and came home with her silly yellow hairstyle jumping with headlice.

'Aren't they sweet?' she said. And they were, Rok – nearly as charming as the adorable flies that buzz around our food and drains all day.

It's no wonder the Emperor's favourite wife is so keen to have some. When you look at them closely, their mouths are perfectly adapted for piercing skin and sucking blood, and neatly retract into their heads when not needed. They have six well-designed segmented legs, and claws for gripping Earthling hairstyles, which they can zoom along very fast.

'Did you get any more smelly socks?' Farty asked.

'No,' I said, sadly. 'I've heard Earthlings do hang out their socks on bits of string in their gardens, which makes them easy to collect, but it's too cold now. Anyway, then they would only smell of soap. No use for the Emperor's wife's perfume. We need socks straight from the Earthling.'

'I've found out something very exciting,' Farty

told me. 'It's not just us and Body Snatchers who can transform themselves into other species. Creatures on Earth can do it too. There are rats who pull a vegetable called a Cinderella pumpkin, but when a furry godmother waves a stick over them saying "*Abracadabra sharazoom*", the rats turn into horses.'

'It's like *The Frog Prince*,' I said, and told her the history.

'Let's go and kiss our frog. The Emperor would LOVE to have a baby Earth king,' said Farty.

But Henry the hippo did not want us to kiss his frog. 'You need a boy frog to make a prince,' he said. 'And my wife is not a boy, are you my little frogletty?' He turned to his wife and flapped his hippo lips all over her. She did not turn into a princess. Instead, she curled into a ball croaking, 'Go away, you stinky old hippo.'

We left them to it, sneaking outside and over the

fence to Colin Snell's garden. We'd seen frogs in his pond before.

Sure enough, two frogs were chatting there.

'You do it. It needs a female,' I said, pushing Farty towards the frogs.

'No, YOU do it. It'll be good practise for kissing Susan.'

'Why would I want to kiss an ugly Earthling?' I asked.

'I didn't say you wanted to kiss an ugly Earthling,' said Farty. 'I said you wanted to kiss Susan.'

'That's not true,' I said.

'Is.'

'Isn't.'

'Is. Look, they're hopping away – quick!'

Farty snaked out her anterior tentacle, scooped the first frog to her Earth lips and made a wet flapping sound. The frog remained a frog.

'You're not doing it right, silly,' I said, sucking up the second frog with my front whirler.

I clenched my Earth lips as best as I could to make a kissing shape. I thought the frog would be slimy but it was cool and smooth. Its pleasant green colour reminded me of my third mummy back on Faa.

The frog sat in my whirler looking bored, so I used my inter-species translator. 'I was told if I kissed you, you might turn into a prince,' I said to it.

'What a lot of old rudup,' the frog said. 'I stopped believing in all that when I was still a tadpole.'

'Maybe it needs to be a human kiss. We'll ask

Susan,' said Farty as we went back to our dwelling.
She opened Mama's special stores cupboard.

Forks,
Brushes,
Trousers.

Meringues,
Envelopes
Pants,
Soup.

Cardboard,
Jelly,
String,
Fur.

Rope,
Beans,
Batteries,
Apples,
Vests,
Padlocks.

Sellotape
and
Cabbage.

Paperclips, Bananas,
Sticking Plaster,
Fish Paste, Jam.

Nettles,
Balloons,
Bandages,
Custard.

Carrots,
Glue, Pins,
Turnips,
Sand.

Mama has taken the trouble
to make our cupboard neat and
tidy like a normal Earthling.

'What are you doing?' I asked her.

'If we bury a gripperful of beans, a beanstalk will grow. It will lead us to an Earthling giant who could squash the Body Snatchers.'

I had no idea what she was talking about until she told me another history she'd learnt at play-group, about a brave Earthling boy called Jack and his beanstalk.

We found two tins of 'baked beans'. I opened one with my vanadium cutter, dug a hole in the earth by the shed, poured the beans into it, put the earth back on top and patted it down. Farty suggested it might help to bury some with their shell on, so we buried the other tin with all the beans still inside.

'There'll be a beanstalk there tomorrow,' said Farteeta. 'Perhaps we can climb up it all the way to Faa and get out of here even faster.'

'Oh I wish we could,' I said, picking up a stick from a tree vegetable on our way inside.

During our search in the kitchen, Farteeta had recognised a Cinderella pumpkin so we thought we would try

Farty says the beanstalk will look like this.

to make a transport out of it. We waved the stick over it and said *'Abracadabra sharazoom'* just like the furry godmother – but it stayed a pumpkin.

'We need rats,' said Farty, zooming upstairs to get some from my bedroom. We restored the rats to their usual size with the Shrinker and then tied them to the pumpkin. This wasn't easy, because the rats got cross and tried to bite us.

'What do you expect? I'm a rat, for goodness' sake,' one said to me when I complained. But finally we managed it.

ABRACADABRA!
SHARAZOOOM!

'Oh, it looks just like the picture in my teacher's history book,' said Farteeta happily, waving the stick again. '*ABRACADABRA, SHARAZOOM.*'

The rats took fright and ran outside into the bushes, pulling the pumpkin with them.

'They're supposed to turn into horses!' shouted Farteeta. 'It's not fair. Why aren't all these Earthling histories true?'

We went to bed very confused, Rok. Could these histories have once been true, but not any more? Maybe visitors from another galaxy, just like us, experimented on Earthlings long ago, so that they lost their transforming powers, and evolved from then on without them.

There's nothing in Professor McSquared's book about Earth that explains it.

Farty went to her bedroom, but I couldn't sleep for the bleeping and droning noises from the 'Command Centre' which Bert calls the cupboard he now shares with Bertina. It went on so long, I finally got up and knocked on their door.

'`Become disorientated`,' Bert said to me. '`Assume off-course trajectory`.'

'Hey, don't tell the poor kid to get lost, Bert,' said Bertina, opening the door. 'We're all in this together, dahling.'

'I'm sorry to interrupt,' I said, 'but why are you making so much noise?'

'The computers have picked up a weirdo blip,' Bertina said. 'We have no ID for it, but it ain't like anything we've seen before. And as quickly as it appeared, it's gone again. We guess it could have landed somewhere on the planet.'

'Do you think it's the Body Snatchers?' I asked.

Bert started bleeping and whirring and flashing lights, but Bertina was calm as ever.

'Could be,' she said. 'We'll keep monitoring it. Maybe don't tell the others yet.'

I went back to bed, feeling strange, though messaging you has made me feel better, Rok. I wish you were here to talk to about it. I'm sure between us we could come up with an answer, just like we always used to.

Yours investigatively,

Flowk

I just got this letter by hyperpost:

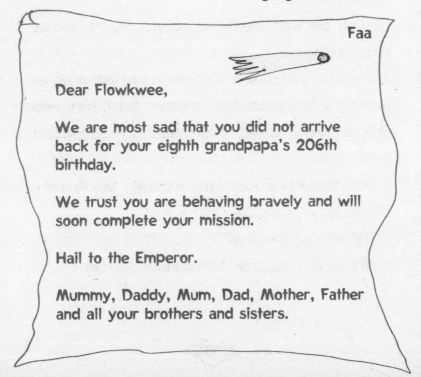

Faa

Dear Flowkwee,

We are most sad that you did not arrive back for your eighth grandpapa's 206th birthday.

We trust you are behaving bravely and will soon complete your mission.

Hail to the Emperor.

Mummy, Daddy, Mum, Dad, Mother, Father and all your brothers and sisters.

Dear Rok,

My mission with Susan has happened, and it was amazing!!!

I met her at midnight on the window-ledge of her bedroom. She looked very excited, her brown eye-balls shining in a way that made all my stomachs melt.

'It's like Peter Pan and Wendy,' Susan said, climbing on to my back.

'What's that?' I asked.

'It's a story,' she said. 'What's in those bags?'

'The Shrinker,' I said. 'We must capture – I mean invite – two people from each of the 205 countries on Earth. If we shrink them small enough, all 410 of them will easily fit in two rucksacks.

'Have you got food and water for them?' Susan asked anxiously.

'Of course,' I said. I didn't mention I also had a can of *Koma*, which would make them happily sleepy, so they wouldn't fight when they were jammed in together. Bertina warned me that Earthlings of different kinds often don't like each other. I've no idea why not.

I sprang vertically upwards at first, and we were soon high above Earth, with Susan squealing in excitement. It was exhilarating for both of us to be looping and floating free of Earth's puny gravity.

We began to orbit the planet, sometimes swooping very close to the surface, sometimes just below the clouds, although I couldn't go too high

in case Susan got cold, or couldn't breathe.

I had to admit there was much that was beautiful about Earth – not just the snowy mountains and ice caps and oceans and dense green forests teeming with birds and animals, but palaces and temples and great cities you wouldn't imagine feeble Earthlings could have built.

But there are Earthlings without houses or

crammed in groups into spaces smaller than my Earth bedroom while others have castles like the one in *The Frog Prince* all to themselves.

Then there are Earthlings without food or water

Some Earthlings inhabit castles,
whereas others live in huts made of straw
that are smaller than Papa's shed.
Some dwellings are made of ice and some
of tin. Rich Earthlings often give their
vehicles large dwellings, and their pets too.

when others have more than
they could ever eat or drink.
Worse, there were lots and lots
of Earthlings shredding each other with terrible
weapons. They'd certainly be better off on Faa.

But although they live in
many different dwellings, eat
many different foods and play
many different musics, not a
single Earthling seems clever
enough to realise how good
it is to sleep upside down. Their brains obviously
do not get enough blood and
oxygen to think as clearly as
we do.

We flew
further and talked to all the people
and animals we met. I had my
portable micro-translator,

so Earthling languages were no barrier to me. Susan looked at me with her admiring look as I talked in all the different languages, so I felt happy.

I also found myself surprised at the variety of rulers on Earth. We Faathings have only one Emperor; they have many, and they're ruled by kings and presidents and prime ministers and dictators and leaders of all different kinds. Some leaders – though not many – are even females.

Some very rich Earthlings seemed sad, despite their big dwellings and vehicles and toys, and some seemed happy without much of anything. Others were sad because they once had plenty of dwellings and toys but had them taken away – like Hiram and Jane, two nice people from America. Their things were stolen by a bank, and they now lived in a box on wheels called a trailer. (I noticed they talked very much like Bertina and Adam One. Susan told me this is called an 'American accent'.)

It is very strange, Rok, but Earthlings seem to believe that 'poor' people need less to eat than 'rich' people.

↑ A week's food for four 'poor' people.

A day's food for four 'rich' people.

I told them about Bertina's 'bank' and how it would give them all the money they wanted, and they seemed very interested in that.

But Jane became anxious about meeting two hairy people dressed like English beds who we captured from Afghanistan. 'Don't put us in with those terrorists,' she said.

The hairy bedclothes said they weren't terrorists, and when I asked what terrorists were, he explained that they were Earthlings who want to explode other Earthlings until everybody believes the same things as them. Since a lot of the people the terrorists were arguing with would presumably then be in bits, I couldn't see the point of this.

'What a strange way to run a planet,' I said as we flew on. 'We all get along very well believing the same things on Faa.'

'Well, maybe that's because you are all scared of the Emperor,' said Susan. 'Maybe he doesn't let you think for yourselves. He probably memory blasted you all so you couldn't remember any other ideas but his.'

Oh dear, Rok. Do you think this could be true?

'You *are* telling everyone they are helping with world peace? And will become millionaires?' Susan asked anxiously. 'And making sure they're comfortable in the bags and not getting squashed? Some of them don't seem very happy.'

'Of course,' I said, although I couldn't be bothered most of the time. Luckily Susan's pathetic Earthling ears could barely hear their tiny voices and, like so many English Earthlings, she only speaks one language and so couldn't understand much.

It was true that some of the people weren't that happy about being shrunk and taken away. Perhaps they do actually enjoy their pointless lives and are fond of their families just like we are.

The more we travelled, the more things I discovered – alphabets, for example. I've said before how limiting it is of English to only have 26 measly letters, but there are many thousands of

Although bears are more dangerous than burglars . . .

letters (they call them 'characters') in Chinese writing.

The animal species continued to astound us. In China there were pandas, moose and black bears which are terrifying, violent creatures. It is strange that Earth younglings cuddle toy bears at night. If they were real, the 'teddies' would bite off their heads.

'Some Earth scientists estimate that 30,000 plants and animals are disappearing from Earth every year,' I told Susan.

'Oh, that can't be true,' said Susan, looking as if she might be about to cry.

I cheered her up by taking a detour to visit the Galapagos tortoises.

'Oh!' squealed Susan. 'This is where a clever man called Charles Darwin started to discover that we all developed from monkeys.'

I didn't like to tell her that Darwin (along with so

. . . most younglings prefer to cuddle teddies at bedtime.

many of the other 'geniuses' on Earth) had in fact come from the planet Zargon. Zargons have been visiting Earth for hundreds of years. Leonardo da Vinci (an Earth 'artist' and 'inventor') and William Shakespeare (who learnt how to mimic and improve Earth 'plays') were also from Zargon.

Well, Rok, we flew home with over 400 people and about 50 new animals to add to the ones we already had. I dropped a very tired Susan off on her windowsill.

'Nigel,' she said, 'you will promise me that you're going to look after all those people properly and give them space to run around and nice food? And don't put people together who don't like each other.' She then insisted on looking closely into the bags, but luckily the *Koma* was working and every-one seemed dreamy and peaceful.

'Oh, they do look happy,' she said, gazing at me with a look that made my hearts somersault. 'I think you're wonderful. Perhaps we really will have world peace forever.'

'Oh, it was nothing. Any time,' I replied. But I flew home with my heads whirling.

'Holy smoke!' said Bertina when I showed her my bags full of tiny people. 'That's swell – we'll have loads to give to the Emperor.'

Unfortunately, some of the little people who understood English had woken up and started shouting and crying for their families when they heard Bertina. What fusspots they are. I'm afraid I was forced to employ a double dose of *Koma*.

Must now get an hour's sleep before school.

Your friend in science,
Flowk

Dear Rok,

Today, Mama was up early preparing tea for the parents of Farty's friends. She's hoping to persuade them to bring everyone they know round on Saturday, so they can all be Improved.

In between her film star magazines, she has still been studying Professor McSquared's *Guide to Earth*, even though I keep telling her it is 70 years out of date. She has been ordering 'party games' and toys and a clothe called a 'pantomime horse' which she wants Papa to wear, to amuse the younglings.

But Papa doesn't want to. 'It is bad enough disguising myself as a two-legged Earthling with almost no intelligence,' he complained. 'A horse has even less intelligence in a head four times the size and which looks like a badly made Earth sock.'

'At least it eats grass,' Farty said, 'not pets like Earthlings do. Maybe it's cleverer than it looks.'

Papa gazed glumly at the floppy horse costume. 'Couldn't I dress up as an Earth superhero or a king?'

Poor Papa is feeling the strain of not being in command of his family, the Improver, or anything else. He thinks the Secretive Services really will vaporise him if our Earth Mission fails again. I am determined to get loads more socks and headlice to add to my little people, so Papa can hold his heads up high and return to Faa as a hero.

At school, Susan kept pulling me aside to go on and on about how the little shrunken people were doing.

'Are you sure they've got enough to drink? And a nice place to, you know, go to the toilet and so on?'

Luckily, Farty had thought of that and had taken good care of the little nuisances. I told Susan they were all happy and making friends with each other. In truth, they are asleep most of the time, but Susan has no truth-receptor and believed me.

'So you think we *will* be able to create world peace?' she asked.

'Oh, in no time at all,' I said. I changed the subject as soon as I could, and told her that I thought Miss Barn's exciting history about *The Frog Prince* may not have been totally true.

'It wasn't history,' she said. 'It was a fairytale. A story. *Fiction*. Made up.'

'Made up? Made up of what?' I asked.

'Made up, like out of your head.'

'What do you mean? Made up of brain matter?'

'No, I mean, invented. Using imagination.'

'Invented? Like an engine?'

Susan rolled her eyeballs.

I tried to understand but she kept going on about this thing called 'imagination' where Earthlings enjoy things that aren't real. So she seemed to be telling me that *The Frog Prince* was not a true story but a LIE. Why would teachers lie to younglings? And if 'fiction' is a lie, then why would Miss Barn tell me I was reading too much science fiction? Science is true.

Is it possible that this history is not TRUE?

'Has the penny dropped?' Susan asked.

'No, I don't have any pennies,' I said. 'You know I don't need money.'

'Oh you are hopeless,' she said, tossing her hair-style and running off to play with Annie Spratt, leaving me feeling so alone.

However my magnifying eyeball spotted some excellent headlice hopping about in the hairstyles of a group of girls in the playground. I got as near to them as I could and bent my Earth head in their direction, but the girls started squeaking, 'What do you want, weirdo?' and 'Yuk!'

'I'm only after some of your very fine headlice,' I said. 'Won't you share them?', and they squealed even louder and ran away. I could feel some of their headlice hopping about happily on my Earth hairstyle though, so by the time I found Susan by the school gates later, I had cheered up.

'You really put your foot in it there,' Susan said when I told her about the headlice.

'No, I did it all with my one Earth head,' I replied.

Susan said that it is never polite to enquire if someone has headlice. There is, of course, nothing about this in Professor McSquared's hopeless *Guide to Earth*. I am resolved to write a superior version so that other aliens visiting this inhospitable planet cannot be made to feel as foolish as I do.

When I got home, my ear trumpets were assaulted by a horrible racket – like *blooglewurgs* gobbling *fluits*. Farty's little friends from playgroup were swarming all over the living room.

Small Earth younglings are strange creatures. Their parents have no control over them.

I only told him to put on his hat

They are scared of adorable creatures like spiders.

NOT *LIKE IT!*
Want **PINK** one!

And they have very poor language skills.

Their favourite word is 'NO'.

NO!

Cabbage biscuits

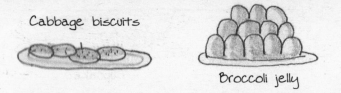

Broccoli jelly

Mama had somehow installed a playground slide, a trampoline and a swing in the middle of the room and several adult Earthlings were looking at them, all holding kettles full of tea in one gripper and plates of Mama's cabbage biscuits in the other. I was just thinking how sad it was for them to have only one mouth (so they can't eat and drink their 'tea' at the same time), when Mama started introducing me to her 'handsome and intelligent new friends' Maureen, Camilla, Bill, Tanika and Emmeline.

I extended my right gripper for the peculiar Earthling habit of 'shaking hands', which I'd never tried doing before. My first attempt was too power-ful and made Maureen squeak, my second lifted Bill into the air, and my third (because I was getting stressed by this time) was an unintentional full-length extension which pushed the very large Camilla on top of the very small Tanika.

Their combined weight tipped up Tanika's chair,

fish and orange sandwiches

Cupcakes

which I was interested to see had wheels on it, like an Earth vehicle. Tanika lay flat on her back waving her little arms as if she were an Earth beetle, while Mama frantically mopped at her face with a lettuce.

'You shouldn't have those silly wheels,' said Mama. 'That's why your chair tipped over.'

'Ten thousand apologies, madams,' I said. 'I am heartbroken if I have offended you.'

'Oh, no harm done,' said Camilla, settling Tanika back in her wheeled chair and offering her a kettle. 'Boys will be boys. But may I ask you to please remove the guns from the play area? I never let my darling twins play with guns. They are so much more gentle than most boys.'

'Oh, but Earthlings – I mean you – are always shooting each other,' shouted Mama. 'Look, they LOVE the guns.'

It was true, Camilla's 'twins' (who looked exactly

the same as each other, Rok) had guns in each gripper and kept saying,

'BANG BANG, you're DEAD.'

'Twins' are two Earthlings born at the same time. Some are identical which means they look exactly alike. Why do their mummies dress them in the same clothes to make it even more confusing?

'Oh perhaps it's all right, just this once,' said Camilla. 'They're such imaginative boys. Look how cleverly they pretend to fight.'

She was distracted by Tanika who appeared to have a bad Earthling 'cold'.

'Goodness, what interesting tea,' she spluttered. 'Is it herbal?'

'Yes,' squawked Mama, 'it is made from brussels sprouts and bananas.'

Everyone tried smiling, but somehow they still didn't look very happy.

'What a fascinating room,' Camilla said, staring around. 'Such an original idea to have, erm, clouded glass in your windows.' (I think she meant the cow juice Mama had used to clean our portholes.) 'Your carpet seems to be made of astro turf and your lighting looks just like belisha beacons. And are those portraits of scorpions and anteaters on the walls? How alternative!'

'And may I say your gorgeous gown is also very alternative,' shrieked Mama.

'Oh,' said Camilla. 'You don't think it makes me look fat?'

'It does, it does, wonderfully fat like a sweet pig. And it is such a nice pink colour, also like a pretty pig. It displays your excellent, enormous chest bumps so well – they almost seem to be falling out.'

Camilla reached for her coat.

'Oh, are you cold?' squealed Mama. 'It is such splendid fun meeting so many elephant, I mean, elegant, handsome mummies. Some of you could be film stars if only you could make your big, puffy bottomy bits smaller. Do have some tulip-flavoured meringues,' she added, whirling to scoop up a small girl with an orange hairstyle. 'What's your name, dearling?' she asked. 'What pleasant fruity hair you've got.'

'Oh I hate it,' said the toddler. 'I wish mine was like hers.' She pointed at Farty.

'But your hair is lovely and oily and thin compared to Farty's. Would you like some of her adorable headlice to make yours even prettier? She's got ever so many.'

'My Earthling name's Sultana, remember? And they don't like lice!' hissed Farty furiously.

Mama thrust a machine gun and a plate of Marmite jelly at the now weeping toddler saying, '*So* sorry, I forgot what cry babies you all are. Now do tell me, which is your mummy?'

'She . . . she ran away with the postman,' sobbed the youngling. 'My daddy brought me.'

'Well, that can't be true, daddies don't bring younglings to tea,' insisted Mama. 'Anyway, I expect you have plenty more mummies, don't you? How many have you got?'

Farty pulled the toddler away. 'Get Mama to

shut up somehow,' she said to me quietly. 'Otherwise there's no way these Earthlings will bring all their friends here to be Improved.' She herded all the little kids upstairs to her bedroom.

I desperately tried to think of a way to stop Mama, who was now suggesting the parents play 'Pass the Parcel', when I heard a cry from upstairs.

'Eugh! A smelly sock mountain!'

Oh no, some of the younglings must have escaped Farty and gone into my bedroom.

'Little animals! And people!' they all started yelling.

'No, no, that's just Nigel's toy farmyard and soldiers,' I could hear Farty shouting. 'Come away into my room.'

'But they're real! And they're growing!'

Then, with a tremendous crashing and banging, a full-size horse galloped down the stairs, its hair-style flowing, its eyeballs rolling. It hurtled across the living room and leapt through the porthole, scattering glass. Oh no! It was Blackie, Susan's pet! Mama tried to calm down the screaming parents, saying it was part of her special entertainment.

I zoomed upstairs swigging a double dose of *Vom*. How could I have been so stupid as to forget to shrink the animals this morning? And I should have checked with Farty how long the effect of the Shrinker lasted on humans. Two full-sized leopards were prowling about on the landing, and the elephant's long curly beak was appearing through my bedroom door, followed by Jane the nice American and a furious man in a fur hat.

'Help! He's a Russian spy! He's got a poisoned umbrella!' shrieked Jane as I grabbed the Shrinker and fired it at them – but horrors! They started *expanding* even more! The little kids all jumped up and down shrieking.

Farty raced from her room, shouting, 'It's still in

reverse mode, you *snortblurking* nincompoop.'
Wresting the Shrinker from me, she reduced the
animals and people in seconds, but not before a
rabbit the size of a cow had hopped over her head
and down the stairs, crossed the living room in two
springs, and disappeared out through the kitchen.

'That wasn't a horse, was it?' I could hear Tanika asking Mama in a faint voice, as Farty and I herded the playgroup kids downstairs.

'Er, it was a special genetically modified one with acting skills for our entertainment,' Mama said. I was proud of her quick thinking.

'It was a giant rabbit, I'm positive,' whispered Camilla, mopping her head and staggering towards the kitchen muttering she needed a drink.

Meanwhile, the horse had stopped running and was quietly chewing the grass on the 'front lawn'. The kids all ran outside to stroke it. Farty and I looked for the rabbit in the back garden but it had vanished.

'It must have hopped over the fences, but at least it won't eat anyone,' said Farty, firing the Shrinker around the garden just in case.

Then I heard an anguished squeak, like a *fluit* stuck in a vaporiser, and felt something squishy under my foot. I looked down and recognised the

£ £ £ £ £

luminous pink of Camilla's piggy dress.

'You've squished her!' said Farty in horror. 'She must have been caught in the Shrinker's beam. We'll be captured by the Earth police for murder.'

She reversed the Shrinker to expand the squeaking Camilla, who was bent into a strange shape even for an Earthling. I shot out all my extenders and grippers and pulled, twisted and pummelled her, and in a moment she was as good as new. She was staring at my extenders with her mouth wide open, so Farty memory-blasted her before she could scream.

'Poor you, you must have banged yourself on the kitchen door,' said Farty, stroking her arm and offering her a glass of water.

'Thank you, my dear, so kind,' said Camilla, rubbing herself and muttering something about how Mama couldn't be so bad after all if she had such polite children.

Just then, Papa pranced in wearing his pantomime horse costume and neighing, and all the parents laughed – rather rudely, I thought.

'Papa's done that to remind you what ordinary, boring entertainers are like,' Farty quickly said, 'but now you have seen what marvellous things we can do with real horses and fabulous playground apparatus, and, er, wonderful mechanical expanding Russian spies, we hope you will bring your friends round on Saturday, when all your dreams will come true. Because not only will we be playing exciting games like this, but we will be giving away LOTS AND LOTS OF MONEY.'

The parents didn't look very convinced. I'm afraid Mama has been just a bit too daft for them this time – and I'm not sure the horse helped. On the bright side, the kids all said they'd had the best time ever, so maybe they'll persuade their parents to come back.

Camilla told us she had phoned her husband to come and collect her and the twins, saying she felt 'a bit wobbly'.

'Of course you do, with your enormous wobbling belly,' said Mama.

'What did you say?' hissed Camilla.

'Oh, she said we'd all of us been gobbling jelly,' said Farteeta quickly.

Luckily, at that moment, a long shiny car screeched to a halt outside, and Camilla's husband came in. He immediately pressed his lips to Mama's gripper in an Earthling kiss. Mama flapped her eyeball lashes up and down like a fly's wings.

'Are you all right?' asked Papa.

'She's more than all right,' said Mr Camilla. 'You must be the owner of that gorgeous Cadillac outside,' he said to Mama. 'Has anyone told you that you're the dead spit of Marilyn Monroe?' He stared deep into Mama's flapping eyeballs.

'You mean the famous film star?' said Mama, wiggling wildly like an Earth worm. 'The one with those bouncing chest bumps that you big strong men are so fond of?'

Mama has a new yellow hairstyle and 'fishing nets' on her legs. It is her attempt to look like a 'film star'.

Camilla pulled her husband away from Mama. The twins wanted to say goodbye to the horse, but it was gone.

When they'd left, Farty and I examined the front garden. There was a warm puddle where the horse had been eating. My sampling probe quickly showed that it wasn't horse-wee, and it hadn't rained, but couldn't tell what it was.

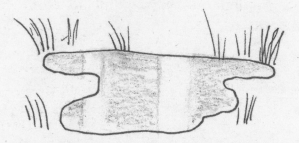

How was I going to tell Susan her pet had disappeared? We didn't tell Papa and Mama either, but we did tell Bert and Bertina, who had just finished fixing the broken porthole and who both bleeped and flickered anxiously.

'Very unsatisfactory development,' Bert announced. 'Quadruped dematerialisation inscrutable.'

'Oh don't be such a drag, babe,' Bertina said, giving him a playful electric shock. 'But you are right. Where has that fleeeeping gee-gee gone, and who or what took it?'

What are the worlds coming to when you hear robots coming out with that kind of indecisive stuff, Rok?

I tried to cheer myself up with this silly game. Try it yourself.

Yours till the end,
Flowk

Put these Earth items in order of preference.
Number them 1-6.
Then turn the page upside down and hold it up to a mirror.
Your WORST item will show up.

ICE CREAM
CHOCOLATE
BOX
CINEMA
BEACH
TV

My Favourites

Fill in the thought bubbles with your favourites...

My favourite colour is ...
Oravaloom

animal
Baby snook (Pluke)

food
Roast jumblies and spoog

game
Fatool

ice cream flavour
I am unable to digest this Earthling 'Treat'

place
Splotoon, Faa Galaxy ZxΣ

song
I very much enjoy all music but have not yet heard enough to make an informed choice

TV programme
Papa does not let us watch TV as he says it will radiate our brains

I had to fill in this worksheet at school.
Unfortunately I filled it in truthfully. Miss Barn
smiled and said I had 'an excellent imagination'.
I am unsure what she means.

MISSION EARTH THREE:
DAY SIX - FRIDAY

Dear Rok,

Miss Barn was 'off sick' today. It was not because of the worksheet I filled in yesterday, but a 'cold' – an Earthling malfunction where they erupt bogeys and sticky H_2O out of their beaks, and their voice boxes sound like the primitive *tar-gurglers* we evolved from squazillions of years ago on Faa.

Our new teacher, Missure Fontaine, said he would 'geeve us a treeet' and show us how to talk 'ze frrrench'.

'Bonjewer, mes ameee,' he said to the class.

This is how a French person looks in Professor McSquared's Guide to Earth. But Missure Fontaine looks like everyone else.

'Bonjewer, missure,' they all said back.

'*Buenos días, señor*,' I said, scrutinising my portable micro-translator. The whole class laughed as usual, but Missure Fontaine looked pleased.

'Ahh, we 'ave a leetle Spaneesh speaker in our midst,' he said. 'Are you from Spain, *chico*?'

I fiddled with my translator and read out what it said. '*Nein, ich bin von einem anderen planeten.*'

The class didn't realise I was saying I came from another planet, but Missure Fontaine understood and thought it was a hilarious joke.

'A-ha, you speak ze German also! Vee 'ave a lingweest in our midst,' he giggled. '*Mon petit,* you disprove ze theory that ze Eeengleesh are rubbeesh at all ze langweedges, even zere own.'

I hid the translator, which had obviously suffered some kind of damage during my round-the-world flight, and pretended I didn't know any more. Susan was looking at me with her admiring look again.

After lunch we joined the small younglings – all very noisy and badly behaved – for a show by the Woopsy-Daisy Puppet Theatre Company. In front of us stood a stripy box in which two tiny shouting people called 'Punch' and 'Judy' suddenly appeared. I never knew Earthlings could be so small without being shrunk. They were also very violent.

Judy asked Punch to look after her baby, but he didn't bother so she bashed him on the beak. Then Punch bashed Judy with a stick! Everyone laughed, but I, being a Faathing brave and true, jumped up to rescue Judy. Susan pulled me back. 'It's not real, Nigel, it's just a story,' she said.

'But he's hurting her, it's horrible,' I cried.

'They're not real people – they're puppets, made of wood and cloth. I'm always forgetting how little you know.'

'That is rude from someone who does not know their 98 times table,' I said. I looked more closely and saw that Susan was right. I'm beginning to see what feeling stupid means myself. But several of the teachers also seemed cross about all the whacking.

Plenty of the little kids at the puppet show had lice, so I picked up another 141 of them to bring home. Now we have 681 headlice altogether (which are making our hairstyles rather itchy) and 206 socks.

I have heard plenty of younglings complain they have lost their socks but the teachers just say, 'Oh don't be ridiculous, you'll lose your head next.' I didn't realise they were detachable.

Susan came back to my dwelling to check on the little people.

Mama was wearing a floaty, white clothe and making strange faces in a mirror. 'I am practising at being Marilyn Monroe.'

We left her twisting her body into strange shapes and found Bertina with her Improver plan.

'Dahlings, the Improver will be ready tomorrow and it will increase Earthling brain power without adding extra heads,' she boasted.

'I think it's disgusting,' said Susan. 'How would YOU all like to be Improved?'

'We don't need Improving,' said Farty. 'You'll understand once you've been Improved yourself and made nearly as clever as us.'

'But we're not Improving anyone this time,' I quickly said, glaring at Bertina. I had already told her what Susan thought.

'Sure, cool it, kiddo, no need to blow your top,' Bertina said to Susan. 'We're making world peace and giving money to the dumbos, I mean, poor.'

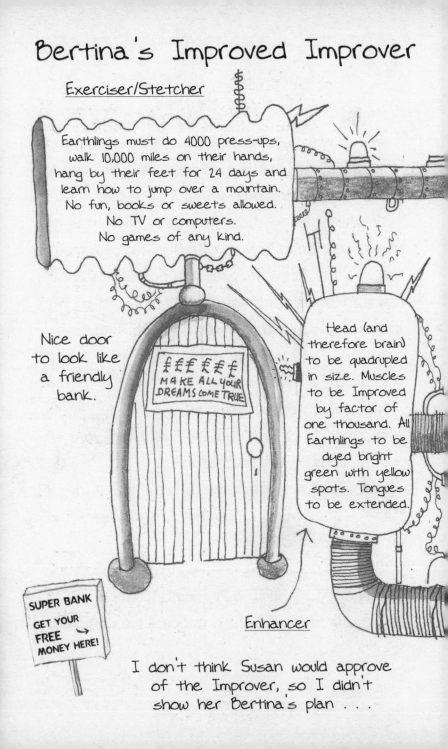

Eliminator/ Scrubber →

Removal of jokes, fun, music, ice cream and cake. Thorough cleansing with wire wool and vacuum cleaner.

Rejection chute for Earthlings who laugh or sing.

Educator

All Earthlings must say, 'Long live the Emperor' in 6000 languages. They must learn to lick the Emperor's floors clean and catch flurts with their tongues. They must know the capital cities in 80,000 galaxies.

Sadlly, rejection is fatal.

Earthling to be polished, varnished and memory blasted. They will now be happy slaves on Faa.

Bleach

Finisher

Nice, new, muscly Earthling slave.

Susan relaxed while Bert gazed at Bertina, his bulbs glowing softly. '**Now there is a wonder that needs no Improving,**' he droned ecstatically. '**Her shiny perspex and titanium casing with its embedded micro-circuitry, contains a beautiful thing – a brain of many colours like a waterfall of wonders. She shines a thousand times more brilliantly than the brightest star. She is a genius.**'

'Jeanses! That reminds me,' said Farty. 'Our teacher told us about this boy called Aladdin who has a magic lightbulb, which he rubbed until a pair of jeans appears, that grants all his wishes. Except I've tried rubbing every lightbulb in the house, and it doesn't work.'

'It's not a pair of jeans, silly, it's a genie, and it's an oil lamp, not a lightbulb,' said Susan. 'And it's just a *story* – of course it won't work. How many times do I have to tell you?'

'What do you mean? These histories are not true?' asked Farteeta. 'Is that why the beans never grew into a beanstalk?'

'Hey, kid, do you understand what "stories" are?' Bertina asked Susan, her circuits fizzing.

'Of course,' Susan said. 'People invent them for . . . for fun . . . '

'They *are* fun,' Farty agreed. 'I really like the bits where we all sit on the mat and the teacher goes "Once upon a time . . ." But now you're telling us none of them are TRUE?'

I put a comforting gripper on Farty's shoulder. I could see she was shocked, but there were more important things at stake. 'Why are you so interested in Earthling stories?' I asked Bertina.

'Because I've just discovered that the Body Snatchers have a dreaded word – gadoodlyblog-glesnacketyfarnschtinker. It means the same as the Earthling word "story", but they're not allowed to say it, on pain of instant death.'

'Why?' asked Susan. 'And what are Body Snatchers, anyway?'

At that moment, Susan's mum rang her. It was bedtime and she was coming to pick Susan up.

'No sweat, kiddo,' said Bertina. 'Drop round tomorrow morning and I'll spill the beans.'

She meant she would tell us everything, Rok.

Susan's mum is a bus driver, and picked her up in her big red bus, which impressed Bertina. 'So it's true Earthlings allow females to be pilots?' she said. 'Maybe they really do have their heads screwed on after all . . .'

I really can't worry if my head might fall off, on top of everything else. I need to sleep, but how can I when I am worrying about the Body Snatchers?

Flowk

Bertina's Improved
Improver is now ready.
She keeps saying, 'It'll
be groovy to see
those dumbos getting a
makeover.'

Hi Rok,

Well, at last we've discovered who the Body Snatchers are.

Susan came round yesterday morning and did her usual fussing about the little shrunken people.

'Why are they all still asleep so late?' she asked.

I shot Farty a look so she didn't mention the *Koma* and we explained that the people had been tired out by the day before, when they discussed how to stop all the world's nations from fighting.

'I even saw the bedclothes peoples hugging the

Americans,' said Farty. 'Now stop worrying, we need to hear about the Body Snatchers.'

Bertina had been doing research and sat Susan and me and Farty in a circle, just like Miss Barn does. Hold on to your heads, here's what she told us.

'Long, long ago, at the dawn of the Multiverse, there emerged out of the collisions of the cosmos two lifeforms. One was a happy, skipping creature who was crazy about jokes, music, science, juggling, roast potatoes and telling stories – a Goody. Unfortunately the other was a lazy, good for nothing, oozy, dribbling, jellified, slob. A Baddy.'

'A Body Snatcher!' we all said.

'You got it. Sad to say they body-snatched the Goodies and became . . . THE SQUELCH.'

'Aaargh!' we all said, clutching each other.

'The Squelch leader was Queen Mandy the Very First.'

'The Mandy Keith was talking about!' I said.

'Quit bugging me, kid,' whirred Bertina. 'Queen Mandy the Very First had 843 baby Squelches. Loads of them met sticky ends – accidentally flushed down drains, falling into their nannies' cups of tea and dissolving, that kind of thing. Mandy the 43rd couldn't sleep because of what had happened to all her broth-ers and sisters. Her jelly-in-  waiting, Effluvia Necrofoomia, told her gadoodly-blogglesnacketyfarnschtinkers or "stories" to help her nod off at night.'

'So she liked stories?' I said.

'Yeah, but hey, Effluvia was cruisin' for a bruisin'. One evening she made a big mistake. She told Mandy the 43rd a story about a cool galaxy-roaming prince in a dazzling silver battle-cruiser who flew over a castle and eyeballed a lonely young queen made of beautiful silvery jelly. Hoping for some cool chit-chat, he swooped too low over the battlements. Unfortunately, the hungry air-intakes of his top-of-the-range cruiser sucked the luckless queen out of her window to perish in the molecular meltdown of the engine. Stricken with grief, the prince flung his machine up out of the planet's atmosphere, becoming a shapeless lump condemned to orbit in the frozen darkness forever.'

'Wow!' I said. 'That's scary.'

'You're right, kiddo. Queen Mandy thought so too,' Bertina said. 'She had her jelly-in-waiting turned into soup and banned story-telling.

'Now, deep inside every Squelch there was still a bit of Goody left, and that little bit of Goody was nourished by stories. So when

This is the only surviving picture from the story
that Effluvia was reading to Queen Mandy.
Bertina says it is of the galaxy-roaming prince.
Susan seemed to like him,
even though he has two heads.

Queen Mandy banished stories, the Squelch became Baddies through and through.'

We all shivered. 'But why are they coming here?' Farty asked.

'Their home planet is warming up even faster than Earth,' Bertina explained. 'Since they are terrified of drying out, they are always seeking planets covered in puddles. They body-snatch the people, snoop about a bit, sleep in the sewers at night and then, if the planet is wet enough, attack, from the sky and from the drains . . . They've conquered fourteen galaxies so far, but are still hunting for an even wetter planet.'

'Oh no,' said Susan. 'Earth is definitely wet – 70 per cent of it's sea. And England is the wettest place of all. At least that's what my mum says.'

'Sure thing, kid,' said Bertina. 'The latest Squelch mission, led by Queen Mandy the 44th, picked up Earth info from stuff left behind by astronauts. They found a teapot, a camera lost near spacecraft Gemini 10, garbage bags belonging to Russian cosmonauts – and their coolest inspiration . . . a photo of a poodle.'

'But it's the most ridiculous looking of all Earth pets,' Farty said.

'How dare you insult my Fi Fi!' barked Pluke.

'Ah, but it wasn't just the picture, it was the words that were under the photo,' Bertina said. '*The poodle is king of the dog world. No dog can compete with its achievements.* Queen Mandy's auto-translator was the problem. It turned "dog" into "god" and "poodle" into "puddle". So she thought the Earth poodle was the God of Puddles. She convinced all the Squelch that only the Great Poodle, if they could find it, could maintain their jellyness for all eternity.'

'But where do the Threggs come in?' Farty asked.

'They need powerful allies. We intercepted this message from a Thregg agent yesterday.'

A familiar voice played from Bertina's speakers.

'HOO HAR. MANDY!
THE GREAT GOD OF PUDDLES INHABITS
THE PUNY PLANET EARTH!
INVADE! DROWN ALL EARTHLINGS
AND LIVE ETERNALLY WITH
PUDDLES AND POODLES GALORE.
HOR HOR HOO HAR!
WE'LL GIVE YOU DIRECTIONS IF
WE GET HALF THE PLANET FOR
A SPINACH PLANTATION.'

'Since then,' continued Bertina, 'we've picked up signals of the nasty Squelch army chanting "Wet Wet Wet", which is their war-cry.'

'Couldn't we defeat the Squelch by shrinking them with the Shrinker?' Susan asked.

'Sorry,' said Farty. 'I've made it work on humans,

but it'll never shrink more complex life forms.'

'But they're just jellies, aren't they?' asked Susan.

'No offence, kid,' said Bertina, 'but the Squelch are 265,000 times smarter than you.'

'I still don't understand why the old queen banned stories just because one was a bit scary,' said Farty.

'Stories are about fun and imagination and dreaming too, and the Squelch never get a chance to do any of these things,' said Susan.

That set me and Farty thinking, because nor do we. We may have superior intelligence and be able to loop and zoom, and have excellent vision on all spectrums, but there are lots of things we don't have: we don't have jokes, or music, or chocolate, or stories. I can't wait to show you all these things when I get back home, if I don't get Squelched first.

We spent today making a new entry for *The Encyclopedia of Predators*.

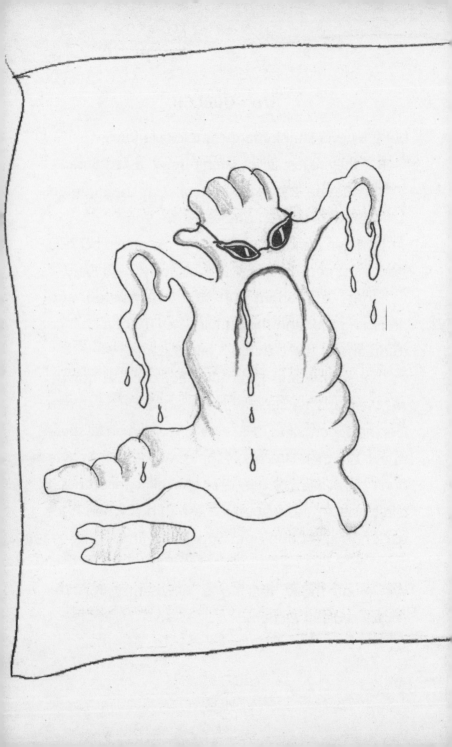

THE SQUELCH

Planet: Gush.

Leader: Queen Mandy the 44th.

Form: Changeable and indeterminate, being entirely jelly and liquid.

Eyes: Fragile. All wear designer sunglasses.

Mission: Domination of watery planets in order to wallow.

They body-snatch important people to check out the planet first and disappear into sewers and drains. They then invade from below (exploding out of drainage systems) and from above (in spacecraft) simultaneously, leaving no room for escape.

Weak points: Unknown.

Diet: Liquid. It is rumoured that the Squelch snatch bodies and suck almost all the liquid out leaving just a small sticky puddle behind. Since Earthlings are made up of about 66 per cent water, they are the ideal food.

Education: Only one book – *The Little Wet Rule Book* – contains Squelch rules, such as *You must obey all the rules* and *Invade a new planet every week until the Great God of Puddles is found.*

So that's it, Rok. The Squelch are drizzling their way towards us now. They will occupy England and the wet kilty bit at the top called Scotland and the leaky leeky bit called Wales and the super wet bit called Ireland on the left – and destroy everything except the poodles. Between them, the Squelch and the Threggs will turn Earth into a puddle surrounded by a vast spinach plantation. There's nothing we can do except collect and Improve as many Earthlings as possible as slaves so our mission is complete, and then get out. The trouble is, no one turned up for Bertina's bank yesterday. I think it's because Mama was so weird at the tea party.

I had to tell Susan about Blackie, too. She noticed he was missing and I admitted I thought he might have been Squelched. She went home in tears, Rok, which made me sad.

Flowk

Dear Rok,

As if things weren't bad enough, horrible Colin Snell made them worse at school this morning.

'The police are coming to see you,' he said, his mouth twisted into that strange shape Earthlings call a 'sneer'.

'Why?' I asked, trying to push past, but he blocked my way.

'Just a few little goings-on at your place that don't add up,' he said, pushing out his chest as if he were an Earthling policeman himself. 'Like that American car outside your place with no proper registration plates. Like a horse grazing in your front garden and then disappearing. Like a monster rabbit hopping out of your house.'

'Who saw it? Your papa on his way back from the drinking-house?' I said.

Mr Snell likes going to the noisy house Earthlings call the 'pub', where you can buy liquid that makes you see things that aren't there and gives you a funny walk.

Colin Snell pushed me. 'Don't you diss my dad, you freak!' he shouted. 'You'll regret it when they come to your weirdo house with a search warrant. So I hope you haven't got anything to hide.' He laughed an unpleasant laugh while I quickly sipped some *Vom* and finally got away from him.

Anything to hide? Only several hundred tiny Earthlings and lots of animals. Plus about 200 stolen socks. Would policemen care about those things?

I'd brought the Shrinker to school so that I could capture Missure Fontaine at the end of the day, to add him to my collection of Earthlings from different countries. But I needn't have bothered, because Missure Fontaine was gone, and Miss Barn was back. She looked as if she should have stayed off longer, though – her eyeballs were even more watery than usual and her beak dripped like a tap.

I was soon about to find out why, Rok, and it wasn't a nice discovery.

I started telling Miss Barn how well my hopping and croaking was going, and how much I was looking forward to rehearsals for *The Frog Prince*.

Miss Barn clapped her grippers over her ears at this, and her beak was now running like a waterfall and making a little puddle around her feet. 'Don't let's talk about that,' she said in a strange, fierce whisper. 'Science, we must do science,' she snuffled. 'We must get on with something *real*.'

She started to tell us about a famous Earth scientist called Thomas Edison who had shown Earthlings how to make electric light. Of course, you know he was a Zargon too, but oddly he liked Earth so much he stayed here. I didn't want to make Miss Barn any unhappier by telling her that, so instead I said, 'Cold fusion would be a

better way to make electricity without harming the planet.'

Miss Barn looked at me very strangely. 'Except that pathetic Earthling scientists will never work out how to do it,' she said in a strangled voice between a snarl and a gurgle.

At first I thought she was just getting crosser. Her furry lines were pointing down towards her beak, which is called a 'frown', and when adult Earthlings do it, you know you have to say something nice to make them 'smile' again.

But this wasn't just a frown. Miss Barn's furry lines were now dripping, like her beak and eyeballs. And why had she said 'Earthling' scientists?

The classroom suddenly seemed cold and, yes, damp. I felt a shiver in all of my tentacles, hidden under my Earthling jumper though they were.

The terrible truth was beginning to dawn on me, Rok, as by now it will on you. But, hoping

against hope, I fired the Shrinker at Miss Barn from under my desk. Nothing happened. She was no longer human!

'I suppose you know that Doctor Filament actually invented the lightbulb first?' I said, and I braced all my tentacles and springers for what I knew was coming next.

'Of course! Every fool in the Multiverse knows that he made the breakthrough at the Warfle Laboratories on EXBox in the year 306739710,' gushed Miss Barn, and water exploded from her mouth, nose and ears.

Annie Spratt started crying. So did Orville Muffin, and he hid under his desk. Aaron Ratchett grabbed me.

'Do something!' he yelled.

Aaron Ratchett has always had faith in me, but right now he didn't understand what was happening, whereas I knew Miss Barn was gone, and a Squelch was in her place. It advanced towards me, with the remains of Miss Barn's Earth face blurring at the edges, slime trailing behind it.

'You should go home, Miss Barn, you're not looking well,' advised Adam Two, whose eyesight isn't too good.

'Is it time to rehearse for *The Frog Prince*, Miss Barn?' Susan asked. I think she was desperately hoping for Miss Barn to return to normal.

The Squelch moaned and flapped its dripping arms up and down, sending gooey stuff flying in all directions.

'Eeeuw, leave it out,' moaned Annie Spratt. 'My mum only bought me this top yesterday.'

'I'd like to practise that bit at the beginning when the princess wanders away from the castle and gets lost in the wood,' Susan went on, waving the pieces of paper with the play words on, at what she obviously still thought was Miss Barn.

The Squelch twisted out of its Miss-Barn shape, gave a horrible slurping howl and wrapped its droopy arms over where its ears should be.

'Watch out, it's a Squelch!' I shouted, and my worried head popped out before I could stop it.

Everyone stared at me in amazement as I swigged *Vom*. Jatinder said, 'So you really *are* from another planet.'

'Oh, it's just a circus trick. That's the real alien,' I shouted as the Squelch gurgled, dissolved into a puddle and dribbled out under the door.

We all chased it as it drooped and flopped down two flights of stairs and disappeared into the toilets. By the time we arrived, it was gone. I swung open each toilet door shouting, 'Where are you, you dribbling, snivelling, clammy, soggy, no-good puddle?'

In the last loo, I was just in time to see the slurpy trail ooze over the seat and disappear into the water. A wet and ghostly voice echoed up:

'The Squelch are coming, you cannot stop us.
We will drown you, dissolve you, sink you,
soak you, drink you, choke you.
I am just one, but many follow.
Your days are numbered.
We are clammy, soft as dew.
We are many, you are few.
And furthermore . . .'

Aaaaargh

I flushed the toilet, listening to the creature's ghastly gurgle of doom. I suddenly wondered what happened to the body-snatched victims of the Squelch. Poor Miss Barn. Had I some- how flushed my teacher down the toilet? Or was her real body still out there somewhere? Could we ever rescue her?

We didn't tell the headteacher that Miss Barn had been Squelched. It seemed too difficult to explain, and Earthlings can be very stupid about things like this. It was the end of the day anyway and everyone just wanted to go home.

I raced back with Susan, trying to dodge the snowballs that had started to fall again.

'*Please* don't tell your family the Squelch are here,' pleaded Susan as we arrived at my house. 'Your dad will panic and you'll all leave. If we just have a little more time, we can defeat them, I'm sure,' she said. 'We can work out how – there must be a way.'

'Don't be ridiculous,' I told her. 'We've got lots of animals, socks, lice and different peoples now. The spaceship is nearly fixed. We just need to get off this lousy planet before we're all drowned.'

'But what about me and my family and Aaron and Roddy and Annie Spratt? What about world peace?' Susan asked.

'You can all come with us,' I said. 'World peace will have to wait a little longer, but it should be easier with less people on the planet.'

Susan stood looking at me, her mouth an O-shape, her eyeballs stretched wide. 'How can you say that?' she said. 'After all we've been through? I thought you had changed, but I see you're just a cold, cold-hearted, heartless, cold ALIEN.'

'You're repeating yourself,' I said. 'And you know we've got four hearts.'

Susan glared at me, before she ran off through the snow.

Females are odd, and Earthling females are oddest of all. But you'll appreciate, my old friend, this was no time to worry about all that.

'The Squelch are here! They've evaporated Miss Barn!' I shouted as I ran into our house, but nobody seemed to care about my poor teacher.

'Who's Miss Barn? Tra la la?' was all Mama said. She was whirling about in front of a full-length mirror, making kissy shapes with her Earth lips. 'What do you think? Could I be an Earth film star? Can you see Bumeflowkmissus from Faa inside a huge, big TV screen?'

Papa was furiously putting back the wires and springs of the spaceship engine, which he had placed on the living room floor. 'That should be working now. We have to find some people to Improve and then we can go home before the Squelch arrive.'

'But they *have* arrived,' I said. 'Didn't you hear me?' I started to tell them all about it – how Miss Barn had been acting more weirdly than normal from the beginning of the day, and got stranger, and how I had tried to shrink her and failed, and how Susan had started talking about the pantomime, and then the Miss Barn Squelch had run off and disappeared down the loo – but no one except Fareeta was listening.

Bertina came in, whirring softly. She never gets excited like Bert does. I think it's because she wasn't programmed to have any feelings. 'Cool it,' she said. 'The Squelch force is still two whole days away.'

'Well it must be an advance party,' I shouted. 'We have to leave now.'

Bert confirmed it. He trundled in with Papa's laptop. 'Listen to this,' he said.

DRIP, GUSH, SLURP, dribble

'WE'VE BODY-SNATCHED
THE PRESIDENT,
WE'VE BODY-SNATCHED
THE QUEEN,
ENGLAND'S PRIME MINISTER
WILL NEVER MORE BE SEEN.
LET THE
DROWNING BEGIN.'

'Quick,' said Papa, 'turn on the TV. If they've really kidnapped the Queen and the Prime Minister, it'll be on the news.' Papa normally forbids television, thinking it irradiates our delicate Faa brains, but this was an emergency.

It was tedious Earth news. The Prime Minister waffled on about how there is no money on the planet, but I noticed he was sniffing. The 'news-reader' announced the Queen had a slight cold.

'I think they've been Squelched,' I said.

'We'd better leave today,' said Papa, 'in case Flowk's right. We don't want to get turned into spinach soup.'

'I'd rather stay on Earth and be a film star,' said Mama. 'Who needs to go home to Faa, tra laa!?

'But if you stay here, you'll be Squelched,' Papa reminded her. 'We have to go NOW.'

Oh no! That would mean leaving Susan without saying goodbye. At last I realised what Susan had meant. We couldn't just leave Earth to be a spinachy puddle. Earthlings are people too, after all, no matter how ugly and stupid they are.

'What about everyone else?' I said. 'We can't leave them all behind to drown. It's not fair.'

'Life's not fair, kiddo,' Bertina said.

'Oh STOP IT!' I shouted, and she was so surprised

her aerials shot out and quivered. 'That's what Earthlings always say when they want an excuse to be nasty to somebody,' I continued. 'Are you a noble Faathing robot or a selfish Earthling?'

'We're in this together, let's not fight,' Farty said.

'We'll have to go back, Flowkwee,' Papa said to me, quite kindly, for him. 'The Emperor will punish me for the failure of the mission – we haven't managed to Improve any Earthlings as slaves – but I owe it to the rest of the family to get you back to Faa alive.'

Farteeta caught my eyeball and I knew she had an idea, Rok. So while Papa's organising everyone for the journey home, I'm sneaking out into the garden with Farty to hear her plan.

Yours,
Flowk

Oh Rok,

I can hardly bear to describe what happened today, but I must try. Farty and I went outside so she could tell me her plan to defeat the Squelch. Many more little snowballs had fallen from the sky, and all the garden vegetables were white.

'We have to be brave and stay,' said Farty excitedly. 'I know what to do. You said your teacher didn't like it when Susan started talking about the pantomime. Don't you see? It was the mention of *The Frog Prince* that made her retreat? Squelch are scared of stories. If we tell the Squelch stories, I'm sure we can defeat them!'

'No Farty, I think it retreated because we'd realised it wasn't Miss Barn,' I said.

'But the mention of a story made it retreat!' Farty insisted.

'You weren't there, Farty. I don't think that was the reason,' I said.

Just then Farty pointed anxiously towards the end of our garden. 'What's that?!'

It was one of those scary-looking white giants you see everywhere on Earth when it snows.

'It's only a snowman,' I told her. 'Made of frozen H_2O. Susan told me about them. They look fierce, but they can't even move.' I dragged her over to it to show her it was just snow.

'Doesn't someone need to *build* a snowman?' Farty asked. 'I haven't built one, and neither have you.'

The snowman suddenly spread its snowy arms and revealed sharp icicle teeth in a horrible smile.

It grabbed Farty, pulling her into its great icy mouth!

'No! Let her go! Let her go!' I yelled, but it just let out a big wet, slushy burp as Farty's legs disappeared from view, and then an even slushier laugh.

'HA HA HA,' laughed the Snowsquelch. 'You next, ridiculous Foathing. Join your puny undersized crony inside my magnificent frozen form. You can be lovingly together, joined in the same block of ice. HA HA HA! When I melt back to my true state with the passing of Earthling winter you will be excreted down the nearest drain. HA HO HEE HEE!'

The Snowsquelch produced an ice dagger from under its cosy-looking, floppy Earthling hat and lunged at me. I sprang vertically out of its reach, and while it was letting out a splashy roar of rage, I zoomed horizontally across the garden and through our back door, slamming it behind me.

'A Squelch is in the garden! It's eaten Farteeta!' I said, my tentacles and whirrers and heads shooting out in every direction.

Mama turned from Marilyn Monroe into her Faathing self in a split second, all four of Papa's heads exploded out and he grew to his normal eight metre height, bursting from his clothes. Bert trundled around bleeping frantically, pouring *Vom* down all our throats.

Bertina insisted we all take off in our spaceship immediately. 'Losing Farteeta is a misfortune but losing all of us would be more unfortunate,' she bleeped. 'We must save ourselves.'

'What about Farteeta? Don't you have any feelings?' I shouted.

'I was not programmed to have them,' said Bertina.

'Well, I'm not going!' I shouted. 'I'm not leaving Farty here!'

'Get with it, dumbos,' Bertina said, 'or we'll all die on this stoopid planet. Take a look outside, and then tell me if you don't want to get going RIGHT NOW.'

The sky was beginning to fill with horrible jelly-like globules. There was no sign of the Snowsquelch, but in the garden, a multi-limbed, many-headed white creature was walking towards the house. It could only be a Faathing.

It was Farteeta, covered in snow!

'Tra la skiddly bop,' sang Mama. Even her unhappy head was laughing, and the other three were singing horribly out of tune. She clapped her tentacles. 'Dearling, dearling, you have returned to us.'

'It worked – they can't bear stories!' Farteeta shouted, as Bertina gave her some *Vom* and she returned to her Earthling shape. 'I started to tell it the story of *Jack and the Beanstalk* before it

managed to Squelch me properly, and it just melted away,' she explained.

I must admit, I was impressed by her quick thinking, Rok.

'We don't know many stories, but Earthlings seem to,' Farteeta continued. 'We'll be armed with more stories than the Squelch can resist.'

I quickly texted Susan. *I am so absolutely sorry. Please bring all the stories you can to my dwelling – telling stories will defeat the Squelch.*

Millions and millions of transparent jellified objects had now completely filled the sky. It would be impossible to get the spaceship through them, even if we wanted to. Wrapped around each of what must have been their heads, was a pair of Earthling designer sunglasses. The ground began rocking. Great fountains of jellified liquid splurted up all around us. The Squelch were coming out of the DRAINS.

'We are wet above,
we are wet below,
we seep, we Squelch,
we drown you wherever you may go.
YOU CANNOT ESSSSCAPE,'
they were all saying, with one wet and hollow
voice.

Everywhere was filled with evil Squelch. There
would never be enough stories to get rid of
them.

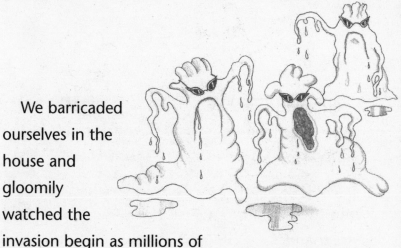

We barricaded ourselves in the house and gloomily watched the invasion begin as millions of the howling, slurping Squelch drifted down out of the dark yet snowy sky. The TV reported that almost as many were surging from drainpipes and man-holes and toilets and sinks. Bert had bolted our bath-room and kitchen doors shut, but it was only a mat-ter of time before a Squelch would come up one of our plugholes. The horrible squelchy, sucking noises were getting louder.

But suddenly they were mixed with another sound. We looked out into the street and could not believe our eyeballs and ear trumpets, Rok.

Three huge red buses were driving down our street, scattering Squelch as they went.

I spotted Susan's mum at the wheel of one. She was holding a megaphone and shouting, 'LET ME TELL YOU A STORY. ONCE UPON A TIME . . .'

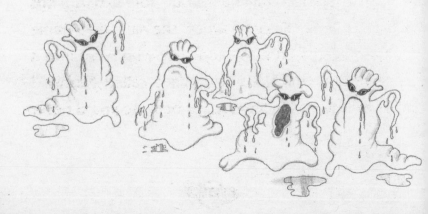

The Squelch reeled back in horror.

The buses screeched to a halt outside our house and about 300 younglings, nearly the whole school, surged out towards us, many of them dressed up as story characters and carrying storybooks. Susan was at the front, Roddy, Aaron Ratchett, Annie Spratt, Adams One, Two and Three, Orville Muffin, Jatinder and even Colin Snell were close behind.

'Hey! Cool! Slaves!' bleeped Bertina. 'Let's get them in the Improver, pronto.'

'No! They'll save us, listen!' I shouted, grabbing Bertina's extender. I opened the window and waved at Susan.

She started talking about four younglings called Peter, Susan – when she said that name she waved – Edmund and Lucy who went into a wardrobe which led to a place called Narnia. I knew she was telling a story because you'd never

find a space tunnel inside a furniture.

The Squelch army, which had been hovering lower again, reared back, and their nasty threatening noises turned to squeakier alarmed ones.

'Arghh! They are telling gadoodlybloggle-snacketyfarnschtinkers!' squealed a nearby Squelch, trembling and hissing.

'*Then fill up the glasses with treacle and ink, and anything else that is pleasant to drink,*' recited Annie Spratt. '*Mix sand with the cider and wool with the wine, and welcome Queen Alice with ninety-times-nine!*'

'Alice Through the Looking Glass, Lewis Carroll, Earth year 1898,' droned Bert.

'Harry Potter met Draco Malfoy, who was actually a Squelch in disguise.'

'Harry Potter and the Philosopher's Stone - misquote,' bleeped Bert, while the hissing and drooling of the Squelch went on around us. 'Squelch reference inauthentic.'

Bertina flung out an extender at him and he ducked and fell on his back. Or front. It's not easy to tell with Bert.

The Squelch were now milling about in the sky and bumping into each other in panic. Still others fled down the open manholes.

Everywhere they heard a story or a line of a story, or a play, or even a story title, the Squelch melted away, dribbling and dissolving. But there were still plenty left, and more coming every minute.

'We need more stories!' Farty shouted. 'What about the little people? Expand them.'

I grabbed the Shrinker, and she and I ran into my bedroom followed by Bert and Bertina.

'Give us a story, Bert,' Farty said, reversing the Shrinker and firing it randomly into my room.

A horse was the first to expand, galloping downstairs just like poor Blackie who'd been Squelched. 'WARHORSE BY MICHAEL MORPURGO,' said Bert triumphantly, flicking through his database. Bert's metallic drone now added the story of *Warhorse* to all the others being read by the crowd from school.

Look, it's Warhorse!

The horse was followed by the fox and as it raced downstairs, Bert mixed in the story of *Fantastic Mr Fox* by Roald Dahl and *The Tale of Mr Tod* by Beatrix Potter.

As other animals expanded, Bert added stories about Peter Rabbit, the polar bear from *Northern Lights*, Dumbo the Elephant, Mickey Mouse, the Three Little Pigs – or Two Little Pigs, in our version.

'Look, it's the Easter Bunny!' cried a small kid from Year Two, clapping its hands. Sure enough, the rabbit who'd expanded during Mama's tea party hopped back over the fence causing a further four Squelches to flee, hissing in fright.

Meanwhile, word had clearly got round the little people and they all shouted tales: 'Ali Baba!', 'Princess Mononoke!', 'Anansi the spider!'

Great holes were appearing where previously there had been a solid wall of Squelch in the sky, and their wailing and moaning was getting fainter.

They were retreating.

'But what happens when we run out of stories?' I asked Susan. 'We're bound to eventually, and then the Squelch will return.'

'Don't you get it?' she replied. 'While we still have imagination, we'll never run out. We can just make them up. There are an infinite number of stories . . .'

I looked at her amazed, realising that Earthlings really can go on making up new stories forever.

'You're wonderful and very clever,' I said. She looked so happy then that I wondered if she was about to give me a kiss until . . . oh NO.

'HAR HAR HOO HOO HAR HAR,' came a voice, and under it a whistling-wind sound as if its owner was travelling very fast.

'HAR HAR AAARGH!'

It ended in a splintering crash and tinkling of breaking glass.

Are the Threggs going to wreck everything at the last minute?

Wish me luck,
Flowk

Dear Rok,

Sure enough,
staring right out
of a small Thregg
cruiser was an oily
purple face, with a
row of six eyes
above a dangling nose
and a set of
of razor-sharp
spinach-green teeth.

Keith, King of Threggs, had shattered the wind-screen of Bertina's Cadillac.

'Bleaking fanookles,' Bertina muttered. 'That's my getaway car.'

'What's that he's putting on his head?' said Susan.

Farty looked annoyed. 'Oh no, it's a music filter. It must be so that if we play him music, he won't be able to hear it!'

'Just thought I'd drop in, contemptible Faathings and utterly ludicrous Earthlings. I have here Queen Mandy the 44th, monarch of all the Squelch,' Keith announced, and followed it with a loud burp in which a stream of fire shot out of his mouth. 'If her whinging, gloopy army doesn't honour our deal to reduce Earth to a ball of slime enriched only by glorious meadows of spinach, I'll vaporise her myself.'

Queen Mandy the 44th gave a wet moan of

terror. The noise of the retreating Squelch got louder again. The thought of losing their queen was giving them strength, Rok.

'Put these on,' Keith bellowed, 'then you won't have to hear their stupid stories.' And he hurled a vast bag from his ship towards the Squelch. In it were millions of earmuffs! The Squelch put them on, and advanced, a vile soaking mass of sunglass-and-earmuff-wearing jelly.

'WET, WET, WET,' they chanted.

I felt a hand pulling at my gripper. I looked around and it was Susan.

'We've got to expand Fi Fi,' she said. 'Remember, they think the poodle's a god. Come on, Farty. Quick!'

We rushed to my bedroom, where Fi Fi was cowering under the bed.

'Expand the dog, Farty!' I shouted at her, scooping the tiny, trembling Fi Fi up. Farty fired the

Shrinker and Fi Fi instantly blew up like an Earthling bouncy castle, but then kept on growing. The portholes of my bedroom blew out, the walls cracked and fell into the garden, the roof split as Fi Fi's surprised pointy face and neat woolly ears burst out into the open.

We clung on to the one floorboard still attached to a tottering wall, before it gave way and we all fell to the bottom of the house – slowing the descent by clutching a huge curl of poodle hair.

'WOOF!' barked Fi Fi, and the noise made my extenders shiver and my Earthling teeth rattle.

WOOF!

The Squelch gasped. 'It is the great god of puddlesssss. Wet, wet, wet,' they chanted, pulling off their earmuffs and gazing at Fi Fi in awe.

'WOOF, WOOF, WOOF,' went Fi Fi.

'She is saying Keith King of Threggs is evil,' I shouted, 'and you've been led astray from the One True Path. She says stories are good and you can be good too if you learn to love them again.'

The Squelch stopped making their horrible sounds and began to form shapes. They became creatures rather like Earthlings, with only one head and four extenders, but they were taller and slimmer, and not such a variety of shapes and sizes.

'Blow me down, they're turning into Goodies,' Bertina hummed quietly, her laser eye-balls round with surprise.

'A miracle is happening,' Queen Mandy said, who was no longer a bad jelly, but a Goody! She spread out her long arms. 'We are becoming the Goodies who

WOOF! WOOF! WOOF!

we body-snatched so long ago . . . It can only be the work of the One True Great God of Puddles.'

'Don't be daft, it's just an old poodle – it's the STORIES that have changed you,' muttered Farty.

The Squelch started weeping with happiness. 'We're Goodies, we're Goodies, tell us a story.'

'Release your prisoners first,' shouted Susan.

A nearby Squelch-Goody gave an enormous burp and out of its mouth popped a dazed Miss Barn! All the younglings ran to hug her.

'Goodness me, what have I done to be so popular all of a sudden?' she said, rubbing her eyeballs.

Several more burps released over a hundred Earthlings. And Susan was very pleased to see her dear pet Blackie again.

'How do they do that?' she asked, running up to hug the baffled-looking horse.

'Who knows?' I said, as more and more Squelch-Goodies belched out Earthlings. The last two to come out were the Queen of England – 'We are not amused,' was all she said – and the Prime Minister.

Keith, King of Threggs, howled excitedly and shot out a tentacle, snaking it firmly round the Prime Minister's neck. He roared:

'HAR HAR HOO.
YOUR VICTORY WILL BE SHORT LIVED.
WE HAVE YOUR LEADER!'

'Yaaay! You can keep him,' everyone cheered as the Thregg craft shot into the sky.

'Don't worry about him,' said Queen Mandy to Fi Fi, as the Squelch-Goodies rose up into space after him. 'We'll see he never lays a tentacle on Earth ever again.'

Just then we heard the sirens of Earthling police cars. It was time to go. There's only so much memory blasting you can do.

'Let's burn rubber,' said Bertina. 'Flowkwee, shrink all them kids and folks and critters and pack 'em in bags for the Emperor.'

'But they've just saved our lives,' I said.

'Oh stop footling about, you softie,' said Bertina. 'If you won't do it, I will,' and she shot out an extender and grabbed the Shrinker.

Farty and Susan screamed as she turned to fire it at all the younglings, but Bert, fizzing and howling, knocked it from her grasp.

'Oh Bertina, my pudding, my own, don't you have any heart at all?' he bleeped.

'Guess not, babe. But it's all the same to me,' Bertina said with a shrug.

Poor Bert. His hopes of winning Bertina's love are doomed if she has no feelings.

'Please, please come with us,' I begged Susan and Roddy.

'You know I can't leave my mum,' said Susan, her eyeballs watering. 'And anyway, I've got to help the foreigners and animals get home. And try to explain everything to the police.'

Roddy flapped his arms. 'Take this,' he said. It was his entire pencil collection.

Now it was time for my eyeballs to water. 'I'll never forget you . . .' I said.

'Me neither,' said Susan. 'I don't want to you to go,' she said.

'We have to, kiddo, else we'll all be put in a zoo by your police friends,' said Bertina, 'or even the jailhouse.'

The sirens now sounded as if they were in the next street.

'Goodbye, dear Farty,' said Susan, hugging my little sister. Then she turned to me. 'And goodbye, dearest Flowk,' she gulped. It was the first time she'd used my real name, Rok, and she looked as if she was about to kiss my cheek. I leant forward, all my hearts looping and whirling, to return her kiss, but it was too late. Bert's extender grasped me, pulling me into the spaceship.

Pluke and Fi Fi and the puppies all piled in on top of me and I struggled to catch a last glimpse of Susan as Bertina pushed poor old Flyzoop aside and pressed the ignition. 'See ya later, alligators,' she said, and whoosh – we were gone.

Papa's hopeless Earthling laptop exploded as we exited Earth's gravity, so I am writing this with one of Roddy's pencils. I know Farty tried to memory blast everyone as we left, but I doubt she completely succeeded since she only had a few seconds to do it. So I guess we will never be able to return to Earth, the planet I once hated, but now quite like. The only planet with jokes and songs and stories . . . and Susan.

I am so sad and I hope I can find a way to send you this before we get home, as I should warn you that although we may have saved Earth, I doubt if you will be allowed to be my friend any more. We have failed in our mission - we have only brought back smelly socks and headlice. Papa is certain to be vaporised. All is lost.

No. Wait. We have just had a message from the Secretive Services.

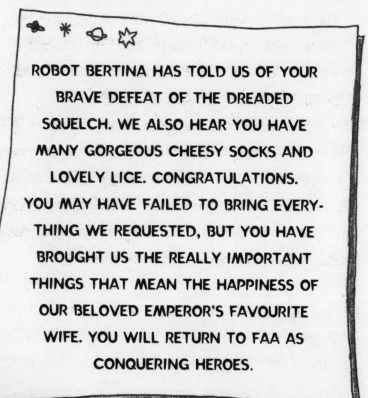

ROBOT BERTINA HAS TOLD US OF YOUR
BRAVE DEFEAT OF THE DREADED
SQUELCH. WE ALSO HEAR YOU HAVE
MANY GORGEOUS CHEESY SOCKS AND
LOVELY LICE. CONGRATULATIONS.
YOU MAY HAVE FAILED TO BRING EVERY-
THING WE REQUESTED, BUT YOU HAVE
BROUGHT US THE REALLY IMPORTANT
THINGS THAT MEAN THE HAPPINESS OF
OUR BELOVED EMPEROR'S FAVOURITE
WIFE. YOU WILL RETURN TO FAA AS
CONQUERING HEROES.

And it was followed by an audio message from the Empress herself.

'I AM HAPPY AS A FANOOGLE AND BOUNCING LIKE A PONG PING BALL. I CAN'T WAIT TO WEAR MY SMELLY SOCK SCENT WHICH WILL MAKE ME THE MOST SWEETLY STINKY WIFE IN THE MULTI-VERSE. AND I CAN'T WAIT TO SEE MY NICEY WICEY SPICY PRICEY LITTLE LICEYS! HOORAY AND DOUBLE HURRAH. MEDALS ALL ROUND.'

So I suppose that's good, Rok. I have a CD and a book and a piece of chocolate to show you. Will they be enough to change the way we live on Faa? Will anyone read these letters one day and think they're a story too? Or will they realise that all this was really true?

See you soon, my friend.
Flowk

Create your own alien,
download out-of-this-world activities,
and read Flowkwee's
galactic blog:

www.alienschoolboy.co.uk

Look out for
the next Alien
Schoolboy book.
Coming soon!

Translated from Alien by
Ros Asquith

ALIEN SCHOOLBOY'S 'Z-A GUIDE TO EARTHLINGS

VERY FUNNY
Jeremy Strong

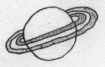